SUGARPLUM

LOVE BEYOND LETTERS

SWEETHEARTS

Other Books by C. L. Fails

Decoding Joy

A Spoonful of Sugarplums

Where Sugarplums Shimmer

A Sugarplum Promise

So Okay...:
Treasured Stories from the Life of James M. Robinson, Sr.

My Magical Story Journal

The Secret World of Raine the Brain Series

The Ella Books Series

The Christmas Cookie Books

SUGARPLUM

LOVE BEYOND LETTERS

SWEETHEARTS

a novel

C. L. FAILS

LaunchCrate Publishing
Kansas City, KS

Sugarplum Sweethearts
Written by C. L. Fails

LaunchCrate Publishing
Kansas City, KS
info@launchcrate.com
www.launchcrate.com

Ordering Information:
Quantity sales. Special discounts are available on quantity purchases by corporations, associations, and others. For details, contact the publisher at the email address above. Orders by U.S. trade bookstores and wholesalers.

Library of Congress Control Number: 2023915108

Hardcover ISBN: 978-1-947506-34-3
Paperback ISBN: 978-1-947506-36-7

Printed in the United States of America
10 9 8 7 6 5 4 3 2 1

First Edition

The highest form of energy is love. It vibrates at the
highest frequency and reverberates in infinite ripples.
Choose love.

We held onto each other for as long as we could - soaking up the feeling of each other's bodies, the scent of each other's skin, the waves of emotion we could feel in each other's eyes.

That was the last time I saw Jackson for a while.

Far longer than we had planned anyway. I was blissfully unaware of the curveball that life had in store for us.

CONTENTS

SUGARPLUM SWEETHEARTS

CHAPTER ONE
MARLEY, AGE 7

The totality of our relationship hinges on one very simplistic fact. The energy you put into the atmosphere always finds its way back to you. I learned this when I was very young and found myself with an extended stay at a local children's hospital, Hope Gardens. A peace dove with a message written by another child gave me hope each morning that I opened my eyes. I didn't know it at the time, but that child would eventually...well, how do I explain the impact that one note had on me? Let's start with the impact of a different note first.

When I was in first grade, I had regular headaches at school. The school nurse said I probably needed glasses. The optometrist said my vision was fine. In second grade, the headaches continued. The school nurse said I needed glasses. This time the optometrist agreed because my vision had changed - drastically.

The glasses didn't stop the headaches, but the people I told about them all thought I was making it up. Then after one embarrassing gym class where I randomly tripped during kickball and then vomited on some poor unassuming kid playing first base, the nurse was suddenly more concerned than when she thought it was just a change in vision. She hit me with a barrage of questions and I answered them as best as I could; yes, sometimes I had trouble pronouncing words correctly, yes sometimes I tripped over thin air, yes I forgot things that I was supposed to do, no I didn't experience any weakness in my arms or legs, yes sometimes the room felt like it was spinning as I was standing still. She sent me home with a note that she made me promise I'd deliver to my mom, "**AS SOON AS YOU SEE HER**," but I forgot.

I forgot that night, and the next, and by the time it had turned into a week of forgetfulness, it had definitely sunken to the bottom of the pile of homework and next great inventions that my 7 year old mind had conjured up on scrap pieces of paper. My Mom, while cleaning out my backpack at the end of the month found the note that the nurse had urgently shipped home with me. The next day I skipped school for a trip to the pediatricians office for a check-up. I stared at a poster of a cat in a shoe and listened to them talk about taking me to a specialist. I didn't know what that was, but I remember turning my attention towards Mom after hearing her voice tremble. It was then that I found myself watching my Mother's eyebrows dance across her face. I remember counting the rows of folds that appeared on her forehead, and I'll never forget watching her unfold and refold that note from the school nurse so many times that the creases began to fray and tear.

After that check-up, we were shuffled off to Hope Gardens to meet with a Dr. Chris, who after hearing my symptoms, extended her day just to fit me in. I remember hearing the words tumor and cat scan. I didn't know what a tumor was, but I did have a vivid image of that cat in the shoe being scanned with a wand, like I had seen at the security checkpoint at the airport when we went to visit my aunt in Chicago. I wasn't sure what that cat scan had to do with me, but I was kind of excited to find out.

They scheduled the cat scan as soon as they could and I was pretty confused when they told me that I was the subject of the scan, and not a cat. They placed me on the table and asked me to pretend I was in a game of freeze tag and be as still as I could be as they slowly rolled me through a big donut that was going to scan my body to help them figure out what was going on. "The more still you can be, the faster we can be finished."

We hung out in the testing room for about 30 minutes or so. Only 5 of that was me on the slow-rolling table. The other 25 was a combination of pre-time and a waiting game to see if I had laid still enough to get a good scan. Once the technician confirmed that my freeze tag pose had done the trick, we went out to grab a bite to eat. That was one of the last "normal" days I had for a while.

Aggressive tumor. Frontal cortex. Biopsy.

I spent days in the hospital as they searched to figure out what type of tumor they were working with. Dr. Chris had called in a specialist for the biopsy and explained to my parents the results.

Cancerous.

After that I found myself in the hospital regularly. Hope Gardens had almost become a second home, I was there so often. The nurses and doctors all greeted me by name. The other patients and I became play cousins after hanging out together in the play area when we found the energy to. It was like one extended family.

My tumor was too large to safely operate on, so they decided to try to shrink it as much as possible with radiotherapy. Check-ups and check-ins. Homework and skipping school. Second grade had gotten off to a rough start, but I held onto the words that Dr. Chris said when we first met, "The world needs your light. Shine it as brightly as you can. Some days it may be more dim than others, but as long as it keeps shining, that's all that matters."

There were days when it was hard to let my light shine. I was sluggish and tired, and I couldn't make my body do what I wanted it to do, which frustrated me. But every time I felt angry, I held onto those words, "...as long as it keeps shining, that's all that matters."

Dr. Chris visited my room every day and cared for my health and well-being the same way that an aunt would. I trusted that she would take care of me the best way she could, so when she told us that it was time for surgery to remove the tumor, I trusted that everything would be okay, no matter what the outcome was.

"I wish I could tell you that it all ends well. Unfortunately we won't know the answer until all is said and done." They were the last words Dr. Chris left us with that night. I didn't know what the next day would bring, but I knew that whatever the outcome, I would be fine. I went to sleep that night resting as well as I could, but nervous that they would be operating on me the following day. That same night my great-grandmother visited me in my dream. I asked her what it was like where she was, on the other side. She told me that time did not exist anymore. They could experience anything they wanted to access in the blink of an eye. There was a feeling of peace, love and happiness that surrounded her - always. She told me that I didn't have anything to worry about, and that I could choose.

Can you imagine that? At 7 years old, hearing that you could choose from your great-grandmother who hadn't been earth bound for almost a year. I was a little bit confused by the dream that I'd had, not only because of the content, but also because I wasn't sure it was actually a dream.

When I woke up that morning, I sat still wondering whether or not that dream was real and curious about the answer to the only question I held. I heard Dr. Chris' voice singing as she peeked her head in the doorway, "Are you ready?"

"Yes, I'm ready!" I sang back to her. And poof, the curiosity that filled me all but melted away.

"What questions do you have for me today Marley?" Dr. Chris asked me.

"Dr. Chris, what happens to me if I don't wake up from surgery?"

She looked me in my eyes and studied my face as I waited for the answer to the only question that was on my mind.

"Well, that all depends on what you believe." Her answer brought a smile. It was confirmation of what I'd heard in my dream.

She got closer to my bedside and I reached up for her face, looked her in the eyes, patted her cheeks, and whispered, "I know you're going to do your best and the rest is up to God."

Dr. Chris nodded and affirmed that she would. Then we crossed pinkies to promise each other that we'd both give our best; me after surgery, and her as she was operating.

My parents came in to sit with me before it was time for us to transition to the operating room. Dr. Chris asked the same question of them, "What questions do you have for me today?"

They shook their heads in dissent. There were no questions they wanted to ask. Dr. Chris gave them a final rundown of the timeline and headed for the door of my room. Dad followed her outside like a man on a mission.

They spoke for a while and Dad returned to the room with a bright smile.

"What did you ask, Dr. Chris, Dad?"

"I just thanked her for taking care of my little girl and giving her best so she has an opportunity to grow up into a young lady."

Dr. Chris disappeared down the hallway. The next time I saw her was during surgery. I felt a cool whoosh and seemingly had tilted out of my body. Beyond the hospital room, where the ceiling should have been, was a bright light. I looked down at my body and then to Dr. Chris, who looked like she was trying to calm her nerves. I peered directly in her eyes, seemingly startling her in the process, then cupped her face and patted her cheeks to reassure her that I was fine.

I whispered softly, "I know you gave your best. Remember, the rest is up to God."

She exhaled, looked back down at the table at my physical body, which was resting peacefully while the rest of the team was talking over each other as they worked their hardest to revive me. I was overcome with peace and watched with admiration as Dr. Chris told every member of the operating team what she needed them to do to bring me back.

I felt the peace and love that my great-grandmother had spoken about. It was all around me. It was me. I was peace and love, and there was Dr. Chris, willing me through her actions back to life - fighting for my survival. In that moment, I remembered her words, "The world needs your light. Shine it as brightly as you can...as long as it keeps shining, that's all that matters."

I heard my great-grandmother call to me, "Remember, you can choose, Marley. We'll be here when you're ready for us." Then, like the snap of a rubber band returning to its home on a stack of mail, my soul snapped back into my body.

I was in recovery for a while, but they read to me - everyone did. I was encouraged to rest, and I did. But I was also ready to get back to normal. There were days when I didn't feel like doing anything, and I looked to the peace dove that was waiting for me when they took me back to my room. It was signed by someone named Jax and encouraged me to give my best, "Marley, you are a fighter. Remember you are strong even when you don't feel like it." That note got me through those tough days; the days when I didn't want to talk to anyone, the days when my body was fighting me.

On one of those tough days, our floor of the hospital was preparing to celebrate the Christmas season. It was the Holiday Jubilee, an annual event. Because I was still recovering from surgery my Mom and Dad decided it would probably be best for me to stay in my room. That was hard. I tried to stay upbeat, but I could hear the music thumping down the hallway. Mom tried to cheer me up by dancing with me, but it just wasn't the same. I decided that I'd rather watch tv instead. While I was flipping through the channels looking for something Christmasy to watch, Mom stepped out into the hallway. She never let me see her looking too worried, but I know she had to be stressed out. When the door to the room opened again, I was staring at a black man in a red suit. As an adult I know better, but as a child there was no way you could convince me that he wasn't Santa Claus. Every fiber of his being was jolly and he even had a little twinkle in his eye.

When he opened his mouth and called me by name, I was almost speechless. Almost. I stretched out my arms for a hug and received the most warm, and tender embrace. I started crying. I couldn't help it. Earlier in the week the nurses said that Santa and Mrs. Claus would be visiting the party. Then all of the sudden, rumors spread that Santa wouldn't be able to make it. But there he was, in my room, and he knew my name. All of that joy bubbled up into tears that streamed down my tiny cheeks. Santa handed me a tissue and asked me why I was crying.

"I don't know, Santa!"

"Are they happy tears or sad tears?" he asked me.

"I'm just so excited to see you!!" I nearly shouted.

"So they're happy tears. Good!"

"They are definitely happy tears! What are you doing here, Santa?" I asked, completely beside myself.

Santa proceeded to tell me about the Jubilee and his pledge to visit each and every one of us at Hope Gardens. I was suddenly full of energy. He asked me about why I was in my room and I told him about the surgery and my spirit leaving my body. He was calm as he asked me how I got back in my body.

"I watched her fight for me and I chose to stay."

He only nodded at my answer, touching a single knuckle to the corner of his left eye.

I had a lot of questions and he seemed to have all the answers. The two of us joked back and forth about his reindeer and how slow they actually are, which is why he drove a truck the rest of the year. After what I'm sure probably felt like a million questions, Santa handed me a book, just for me, "The Story of Santa Claus." No wonder he had all the answers. He had an entire book about himself. He read me the story of Santa Claus and Mrs. Claus and told me all about how each Santa had to choose their own Mrs. Claus.

I looked down at his finger for a wedding ring and didn't see one. "Do you have a wife yet Santa?"

He placed his right hand over his heart and chuckled, "I've chosen one, if she'll have me."

"Where is she?"

"She's out on the dance floor right now, dancing with all of the children," he grinned.

"How do you know she's your Mrs. Claus, Santa?"

"I just know, Marley. I can feel it."

I giggled. "Will you tell me about her?"

"Well, she's kind."

"Uh huh..." I said, while leaning forward in the bed, hugging the book he had just gifted me.

"She's caring."

"Uh huh..."

"She's considerate."

"Uh huh..."

"I can see her soul and I'm positive she can see mine."

"You love her, Santa?"

"Well I'm Santa. I love everyone!"

"Okay, Santa! I'm just sayin. You said you wanted to

marry her."

"I did."

"Are you IN LOVE with her?"

Without flinching, Santa answered. "I grow more in love with her every day that I'm lucky enough to spend with her, Marley."

"Awww, Santa! Yay!!" I squealed. I knew all of the answers to the rest of my questions were probably within the covers of that book, so I got really quiet. Santa picked up on my silence,

"Okay Marley, that's enough about me and Mrs. Claus. What's your Christmas wish?"

"I don't know if you can grant me this wish, Santa."

"Try me, Marley."

"Well..." I hesitated, only because I really really wanted this Christmas wish to come true.

"Well?" Santa asked, tilting his head towards the ground and leaning in closer.

"I want Dr. Chris to find someone who talks about her the same way that you talk about Mrs. Claus." I was serious. No smile. Deadpanned face.

Santa smiled at me, "THAT I can do."

I was taken aback. "How can you be so sure? How can you promise me that?"

"I know her heart, Marley."

I studied his face, trying to see whether or not he was telling the truth.

"Marley, why is that your wish? You could wish for anything in the world."

"She told me about my light. I just want her to have someone who would fight for her the same way she fought for me."

Santa nodded and continued smiling in my direction.

"I can see why she would fight for your light to stay here. You have a beautiful soul, Marley."

"Thank you, Santa!" I was excited but suddenly tight-lipped as I tried to decide whether or not to ask the next question that was hanging out in my mind. He nodded towards me, as if he knew there was something I wanted to ask.

"So, Christmas wishes...do they operate like birthday wishes?"

"Yep. You pretty much have to keep that one to yourself if you want it to come true."

"But how will I know if it comes true? Won't I have to tell Dr. Chris about that one?"

"Tell her at your own risk," he laughed.

That visit with Santa was a much needed boost. It came when I was at my lowest and gave me some energy to make it through that day.

At seven, it was hard to understand why any of my medical challenges were happening, so that visit was timely. That peace dove note that I received from Jax was especially timely. It helped me to feel seen. It helped me to feel supported. It helped me to feel loved. And because of those three things, I automatically loved the person who wrote it, even though I didn't know them. I read it everyday.

On the morning of Christmas Eve, just two short days after my visit with Santa, I was sitting up reading the book he had gifted me when Dr. Chris walked in. I think I caught her off guard because I was reading the book myself instead of waiting for someone else to read it to me. The truth is, that was the first day I had attempted to read anything other than the note on my own, and the sole reason I had attempted to read that book on my own is because I felt so loved when I woke up and read the note.

Dr. Chris was shocked to find me there, reading. I showed her my book and told her where it came from. She cried during most of that conversation and I wasn't sure why. I told her about my chat with Santa. I figured it was the only way I'd know if that wish came true. Tears. I told her about the twinkle in his eye and my Christmas wish. Big tears. I asked her about the author of the peace dove note. She told me his name - Jax, and that he was about my age. More tears followed that. I asked if she could let him know how much I appreciated the message and she told me that she would. We shook pinkies before she left the room and I promised her that I'd give my best that day.

"Merry Christmas!" I wished her before she left my room for the day.

It only felt like 30 minutes or so had passed when suddenly there was a ruckus on our hospital wing. It sounded like someone was running down the hallway. I kept an eye on my door as the footsteps got closer and closer. Before I knew it, I was watching Dr. Chris leap into the arms of a man who looked like he loved her. He held her the way my Dad held my Mom. It was an embrace of protection.

I remember thinking that he looked like he was cradling her with so much love in his soul. With his eyes closed, he nuzzled his face against hers and it looked like he exhaled for a mighty long time. Suddenly remembering my Christmas wish, I squealed. I had just watched it unfold and come true right in front of my eyes. He spun her around in a circle and hummed to her. She sang to him and looked at him like she was praying this was real life and not a dream. Then they kissed and everybody cheered. Dr. Marlo handed them their ciders and Dr. Chris pulled this mystery man into my room to introduce him as my Christmas wish.

He tried to hide his face from me, but when he knelt down and glanced up in my direction, I knew it was him. I studied his face. The twinkle was still in his eye. Santa was in my room. I saw Dr. Chris kissing Santa Claus. That meant Dr. Chris was his Mrs. Claus if she would have him and I had spilled the beans. I hope she knew how he felt about her before I said something. Then I was struck with a question that made my heart drop. If Dr. Chris would have him, if she chose to become Mrs. Claus, would she have to return to the North Pole with Santa? I asked him.

"I'll love her wherever she is," Santa assured me.

"Always?" I asked him in return.

"As long as there is breath in my lungs," he nodded.

I reached out to hug and thank him for granting my Christmas wish.

They left my room and my parents came to visit soon thereafter. They stayed for Christmas and we celebrated together in the common area with the other families.

The energy created from Jax's note, Santa during his visit, and Dr. Chris at every visit, propelled me towards recovery. I don't even know if they're aware of the impact of their actions, but because of them, I felt seen. I felt supported. I felt loved.

My goal from that Christmas onward, was to make sure that other people felt the same way because of the energy I poured into the world as well.

And somehow, I was going to find a way to return the favor to Jax. I didn't know who he was or how to find him. But his words helped me choose the best for myself each day after surgery. I'm sure that helped me to get well sooner than later.

Somehow, some way, I knew I was going to pay him back. That was a promise I intended to keep.

CHAPTER TWO
JAX, AGE 7

What took me to the Hope Gardens on that day was love. No, no. It's not the type of love you think. It was a childhood crush on my friend, Lola that landed me in the hospital. I was involved in a dance off with a classmate who was trying to impress the girl that I had a crush on. He knew I had a crush on her, so he tried to show me up. I was busted by my Godfather, Mr. Charlie, who also happened to be a teacher at my elementary school. It was a wild turn of fate actually. He saw me jump off of a bench at school.

I didn't know that the bus ride home was going to be my last bit of freedom that calendar year. School was almost out for the holiday break and that flip, as it turns out, would lead to me creating a prison of my own making. Had I known that I'd end up in the hospital that night, I probably would've sat across from Lola. I would've worked up the nerve to shoot my shot. Instead on that fateful Friday, I sat next to my best friend and listened to him talk about Roblox. I guess I was interested in what he was creating, but I kept sneaking a peek to see if Lola was watching our conversation. She wasn't. And because she wasn't, I knew I needed to work on perfecting my flip.

When I hopped off at my bus stop, I took a glance back at the window where she was sitting. As the bus pulled away she waved. I waved back and ran to my front door. Before I could ring the doorbell, the door swung open. There was Dad on the other side, with a serious look on his face. "Who were you waving at bud?"

"My friends, Dad," I said as I tried to walk into the house past him. He placed one hand on my shoulder and spun me around.

"I only saw one friend wave, Jax. What's her name?"

I mumbled her name as low as I could, "Lola."

"Hmm? What's that? I didn't hear you, son," he asked while cupping his hand to his ear.

"LOLA! Her name is LOLA, Dad!"

"Who's Lola, Jax?"

"My friend, Dad! I told you, already."

"Is this friend encouraging you to flip off of benches at school?"

"Ummm..." Mr. Charlie, had ratted me out. I didn't know how to get out of this one. I couldn't lie about it, and I didn't really want to tell the truth. So I stalled until Dad let me off the hook and told me the rest of the story about how his flip for Mom left him injured.

I listened to it, but in the back of my mind I knew that I still needed to get my flip right. She was watching me. I went to my room and practiced until I nailed it 5 times in a row. By that time, Mr. Charlie had shown up for dinner.

He was always by himself for dinner. So it was just the

4 of us; Mom, Dad, Mr. Charlie and me. That day was no different. I greeted him at the door, excited for him to see that I had perfected my flip since he decided to tell on me.

"Can I show you the flip Mr. Charlie?" He looked down at me like he was trying to figure out what was going on, then asked me to wait until after dinner. At least that's what I remember hearing him say. So I waited - through dinner and asked when he was going to bring someone over with him. Mom hollered at me. Mr. Charlie spit out his drink before he promised me that he wouldn't bring anyone until he knew for sure that he was going to marry them.

I nodded as the adults tried to shift the conversation and stood up from the table. **BINGO!** It was after dinner. Time for me to show him the flip.

Apparently five times in a row wasn't enough practice to have perfected it. I mistimed it. I knew it when I left my feet. I only remember hitting the floor and the pain erupting through my entire body. I closed my eyes for a split second as Mom scooped me up and started running towards the garage. Everyone sounded like they were running. Before I knew it, we were in the car, zooming down the street. At some point on the trip to the hospital the pain felt like it disappeared. I'm not sure if I just got used to it, or if I blocked it out. Whatever happened I'm grateful. When we were waiting in the hospital I was able to sit quietly, even though we all knew my arm was broken.

Mr. Charlie came with us. He told me to keep my chin up as he left to move Dad's car. They had paged someone named Dr. Chris to meet us in the Family Room lobby. So I waited and eyeballed each and every male staff that approached the space. Before I knew it, a woman with glasses was greeting us and introducing herself as Dr.

Chris. I was confused but in that moment, I learned to stop making assumptions. Totally missed the mark on that one.

As we walked towards the exam room, Dr. Chris told me about the peace doves that were hanging on the tree in the hallway. They all held seeds in the paper and each wish of hope was planted in the hospital garden the following spring. There was literally a hope garden on the hospital grounds and I was excited about adding to it.

That was just the distraction I needed from the fact that I was walking through the hallway with a broken arm.

They took Dad and I into the exam room to prepare us for what was next, then before I knew it, they were popping my arm bones back into place - resetting it closer to how it looked before my ill-fated flip. They wrapped me in a protective cast and let me rest overnight in the hospital after my body temperature had dropped unexpectedly. The next morning when they were confident that everything was stable, they released me from the hospital.

Before we left, I made a beeline for the tree, grabbing the first name that looked like another boy - Marley.

I scribbled in my message of hope and gathered the two doves I'd given to my parents. We were supposed to hang them on a different tree, but I wouldn't leave until we handed them directly to Dr. Chris. Mom knocked on her office door and I quietly handed her the three doves with my non-broken appendage. They scheduled a day for me to return for a check up, just to make sure everything was healing correctly I guess. So we said goodbye, for now and went back to see her in a week.

That was when she met Mr. Charlie. It was the last day of school before winter break and Mr. Charlie took me straight in for my check up. We met Mom in the waiting room, checked in with someone in charge and took a seat in the waiting area. Mr. Charlie looked about as nervous as I felt. He kept fidgeting with his shirt and bouncing his leg while he and Mom were talking to each other. They walked us back to the Green Room and called for Dr. Chris to meet us. Mr. Charlie shifted from nervous to confused when we told him that Dr. Chris was my doctor. He made the same assumption that I did.

When she walked into the room, the two of them stopped breathing for a second. Mr. Charlie stood to his feet and started stammering over his words. I looked at Mom and shrugged. I wondered if that's how I looked when it came to Lola. In that moment I made a promise to myself that I would find a way to be cool when I was around someone that I liked. I mean at that moment, I was in the hospital getting a broken arm checked out because I was trying so hard to impress someone that I lost sight of what was really important. It's funny really, now that I think about it. When I was 7 years old I made a choice to become essentially unbothered by the presence of a crush, even though inside I was as much a bumbling and jittery mess as Mr. Charlie was on that Friday in December.

When we left the room and walked down the hallway, he told us he'd meet us at the elevator. My backpack was still in his truck so I wondered where he was going. I needed that! I turned around, about to ask where he was going but he was already too far down the hallway. So I watched as he hustled back towards the Green Room and he and Dr. Chris nearly collided in the doorway. He wasn't even trying to be cool. I could see him swinging for the fences from all the way down the hall. I looked up at Mom, who was also watching Mr. Charlie.

"Something's up with those two, Jax. I don't think this

is the first time they've met."

I laughed and agreed with Mom then directed my attention back down the hallway towards Mr. Charlie who was taking something from Dr. Chris. He turned back in our direction with a big wide grin on his face and walked towards the elevator. Dr. Chris watched him walk all the way to us with a similar grin on her face. We passed another doctor as we got on the elevator and headed back to Mr. Charlie's big blue truck so I could grab my backpack. Mom didn't say anything to Mr. Charlie about what we saw in the hallway of the hospital. Instead she waited patiently for the two of us to say goodbye for the moment as he handed me my backpack.

Mom and I headed to her car so we could go home. We noticed Mr. Charlie was still sitting in his truck in the parking lot. He was on the phone, smiling the same cheesy grin that was on his face since the moment Dr. Chris walked into the Green Room. I knew he had a crush on her and I told Mom in the car, "I bet he's talking to Dr. Chris!"

We didn't see him that night for dinner, but he did come to Mom and Dad's Christmas Party the next week. I remember him looking the exact opposite of how he looked in the parking lot when we drove away. Mom talked to him while Dad and I were in the other room pretending not to listen to their conversation. It sounded like he was supposed to bring Dr. Chris with him that night and I wondered if that meant he was going to marry her. He said he wouldn't bring anybody with him until he knew for certain that he was going to marry them. So in my 7 year old brain, if she was supposed to be there with him, they were going to get married.

He left in a hurry on that day, wishing us a Merry

Christmas and promising that he'll see us soon. That was two days before Christmas. We didn't see him again until my birthday, January 1st. He and Dr. Chris showed up together and that sappy grin was back on his face. Mom sent Dad and Dr. Chris in to hang with me and Dad while she talked to Mr. Charlie.

I decided to have a conversation of my own with Dr. Chris.

"So you're going to marry Mr. Charlie?" I was 7 and didn't yet understand anything about tact.

"Well, you get straight to the point, don't you Jax? Tell me why you think that," she said, seemingly amused that I was holding such a grown up conversation.

"Well he's always smiling when you're around. He just looks so happy. When he was here last week and you weren't here with him, he was sad."

"He was?"

"Yeah, like REALLY sad. I thought he was going to cry," I told her as she wiped a tear away from her left eye.

"Oh no."

"It's okay 'cause you're here with him now - and he told me he wouldn't bring anyone here with him unless he was sure he was going to marry them."

"Jax! You're just gonna drop a dime on your godfather?" Dad asked me.

She grinned about as wide as Mr. Charlie, "When did he say that, Jax?"

"He said it right before I broke my arm. I asked him why he was always at our dinners alone and that's what he said." I mocked his deep voice as best as I could, " 'I promise I won't bring anyone here until I know for certain that I'm going to marry them,' then dinner was over and I went to show him my flip and the next thing I knew we were zooming to the hospital."

"So tell me about this flip and why you were practicing it."

"I was trying to impress my friend Lola."

"Ohhh, you mean Lola who signed her name with a heart on your cast?" She asked with one eyebrow raised in the air. When Mom asked about the same thing, she had the same expression on her face. Anytime her eyebrow popped like that, it was because she was suspicious. I assumed it was the same for Dr. Chris.

"Dr. Chris!" I could feel myself starting to grin like Mr. Charlie did whenever Dr. Chris was around and remembered the promise I'd made to myself more than a week before that. *Steel yourself, Jax.* I could feel my body shifting the more I repeated it to myself.

"Do you think she needs all of those flips to like you, Jax?"

I shook my head no and quietly answered, "Probably not."

"Yeah, I don't think so either. Let her like you for who you are on the inside buddy."

I nodded as I thought about her message to me. Dr. Chris smiled and passed along yet another message.

"Thank you for the kind words you and your family wrote on the peace doves before you left the hospital."

"You're welcome. Did Marley like the message?" I couldn't wait to hear if he'd said something after receiving the peace dove I wrote to him.

"She sure did," Dr. Chris confidently replied.

"She?" I was confused. I just knew Marley was a dude. I was supposed to stop making assumptions but I guess the lesson hadn't sunk in at that point.

"Yes. She told me she reads it every morning which is

pretty special, Jax."

At that point, Dad slipped out of the room.

"Oh," I was a little bit disappointed that I written a note to a girl other than Lola.

"We just never know what kind of impact our words can have on someone else's life, do we?" she said with a smile on her face.

My little soul was still kind of crushed that I'd almost sort of cheated on a girl who wasn't even my girlfriend. "No, I guess we don't."

"She was very grateful for you," she told me as I started to feel another sentimental grin coming on.

Steel yourself, Jax. Steel yourself.

I'm not sure why the thought of someone being grateful for me made me feel so sappy, but I remember thinking Lola was going to be mine and this Marley girl could not get in the way.

I nodded as cool as I could and Dr. Chris changed the subject right as Mr. Charlie and his cheesin' self walked into the room where we were.

I asked him the same question I asked Dr. Chris when she got in the room and he quickly mmm hmmm'd his way through the answer, then changed the subject. They hung around through the evening and Mom and Dad had a lot to say when they left. They accurately predicted that the two of them would be engaged before the year was up. I on the other hand was left thinking about this girl, Marley and how she could possibly appreciate me so much if she didn't even know me. I didn't know who she was or how I was going to meet her, but I felt like I at least needed to see what she looked like.

CHAPTER THREE
MARLEY, AGE 8

My parents took me back and forth to the hospital less and less as the year passed on. Eventually I ended up visiting once every other month, then every three months, because my body was healing itself. There were lots of changes at the hospital. Dr. Marlo, one of my favorite doctors, moved away. Dr. Chris and Santa got engaged and I wasn't sure if she was going to move away too. But I was beyond excited that they asked if I wanted to be part of their wedding. Were they kidding? What kid wouldn't want to be there to watch the wedding of Santa and Mrs. Claus - and they asked me to be part of it? Sign me up.

It was a week after Christmas, so Santa - at least in my mind, had plenty of time to rest from his global jaunt around the world. It was a magical day. I got to wear a girly dress with a big bow and they outfitted my wrist with a corsage adorned with purple hydrangeas and light red carnations. There was so much snow that I could hardly believe it. It definitely felt fitting for the wedding of Santa and Mrs. Claus to 8 year old me.

When it was time, we all stood up as the doors of the sanctuary opened up to reveal Dr. Chris in her beautiful gown. I smiled at the glow of love that surrounded her and turned to look at Santa - who I also called Mr. Charlie. The ceremony proceeded and there were tears all around; Santa, Dr. Chris, their parents and his grandparents. When I was called to speak, I slowly walked towards the front of the church. It was so quiet that you could hear each and every step that my patent leather Mary Janes took as they approached the box that marked my spot. The pastor held my hand as I stepped up on the box to reach the microphone and asked if I was okay before he returned to the pulpit.

I stood at the front of the church and looked out into the pews. There was one face that stood out amongst the crowd. The ring bearer. A young boy, about my age, all dressed up and wearing a bow tie. He wouldn't stop looking at me. One second he'd be grinning at me and the next his face was stoic and cold. Then in the blink of an eye he'd be right back to grinning. I smiled at him and cleared my throat so I could begin.

I had been given two passages to read, sort of. The first was an excerpt about marriage from, "The Princess Bride." The second passage was something they asked me to create myself. Dr. Chris asked me one question and told me that she trusted whatever my answer was, that the answer to that question was going to come from my heart and it would be filled with goodness and light in the same way that I was. The question, *"How do you love someone forever?"*

My answer:

> "As you hold the hands of your beloved, remember
> that there's more to love than the feelings of
> passion that pull you in close on this day. Love
> is helping each other up when you fall. Love is
> communicating why you're angry and coming to
> a resolution together. Love is holding each other
> through grief and walking beside each other in joy.
> Love is supporting each other's dreams and never
> allowing doubt to creep in or settle in place. Love is
> creating individual pieces that fit together to build
> something greater. Love is walking together in the
> same direction every single day, not because you
> have to, but because you want to, you choose to,
> you promise to. Love is unspoken tenderness that
> adds light and life to others with each passing hour.
> Choose love today. Choose love tomorrow. Choose
> love, always."

That was the answer, to me. Looking back on it now,
I know love feels much more complex as an adult. But
as a child, love was simple. It was something you chose
to show someone. When you love your family, you show
them with your words and actions that you love them.
And if that was true of birth family, it could also be true of
chosen family as well.

The ceremony was short but their first kiss as a married
couple was not. I remember covering my face as they just
kept kissing. Santa was *in* **LOVE**, let me tell you. He held
Mrs. Claus's face in his hands and kissed her like it was
the last time he'd get to do so here on Earth. The passion
and deep love they held for each other was something
I wanted for myself. I knew that whenever I found my

person, I wanted to have that type of unrestricted warmth and affection for each other. I wouldn't take anything less as acceptable.

The reception, held at a local coffee shop - which they said was the place where they met - was equally as beautiful as the ceremony, at least for the short amount of time that I was there. Because their wedding took place on December 31st, not only was there abundant snow, the nights were short and my parents didn't want to keep me out too late. Still, in all that I got to experience, including the bridal party's entrance to "What Are You Doing New Year's Eve?", the meal of waffles whipped cream and fresh fruit, Santa and Mrs. Claus's first dance to "Little Christmas Tree," and their toast with sugarplums in each of our tall glasses of sparkling apple cider, the reception was full of love and a spirit of celebration. There was a sense that embracing each day for all that it brought was worth cherishing - and cherish that day, did each guest do. Including the nameless young boy who was fighting whether or not he wanted to smile or mean mug me. I smiled at him regardless of whatever he felt about me.

I thought he was going to come talk to me, because he worked his way around the room, one table at a time. But his mom swooped in and took him out on the dance floor. When he sat back down at his table, he looked sad. He kept looking in my direction and I smiled each time he looked over, but he wasn't budging from his seat. Then, just as I worked up the courage to go say hello and see if he was okay, Dad came back from the coat check with one for each of us. That was the clear, obvious and universal sign that it was time to go.

We said our goodbyes to Santa and Mrs. Claus and headed out of the reception.

"Marley, you were fantastic today!" Dr. Chris told me as she hugged me tightly.

"Did you write that passage about what love is?" Santa asked me.

I nodded and told him that my Mom helped edit it. They thanked me for sharing their day with them and asked if I got to meet any of the other kids. I told them that I only met Corwin and Christina and they smiled knowingly at me while telling me that I'll get to meet the other person when the time is right.

We passed by his table and I felt a rush of warmth in my belly when I got to look him in the eyes and smile on my way out the door. In that moment, I knew they were right.

Once we were in the car, my parents asked me if I knew the ring bearer. I told them both that I didn't think so, but I felt like we'd met before. They said he looked at me like he knew me, but instead of turning around so we could meet, Mom kept driving slowly until we made it safely back to the house through all of that snow. I didn't know him, but my soul did. How does an 8 year old explain that concept to their parents? I didn't even try. Instead I took matters into my own hands.

Since I couldn't say hi to him in person, I decided to write him a letter and give it to Dr. Chris to see if she was willing to deliver for me. I mean, he was the ring bearer in her wedding. I was sure she had to have an address for him.

Dear Ring Bearer,

My name is Marley and I am 8 years old. I saw you staring at me during Dr. Chris' wedding. I am writing you to tell you that I like your smile. Your face looks kind when you smile but not when you turn your smile off. You should leave it on more often. I like your kind face.

Did you have fun at the wedding? Please write me back.

Marley,
(the girl who wore flowers on her wrist)

That night I dreamt about Santa and Mrs. Claus showing up at my own wedding. In the dream I was older, but the face of the groom surprised me. As the doors opened and my Dad extended his arm, we began our long stroll. There he was, standing at the end of the aisle. My groom, trying to decide whether or not to smile or remain straight faced. When he couldn't decide that I was worth smiling for, I tapped my Dad on the wrist and we turned around and left. I never looked back. Unrestricted warmth and affection was clearly not present and I couldn't see myself spending the rest of my life without it. It was a dream, but it felt so real.

The amount of disappointment I felt still lingered in my soul long after I woke up on that day. I had a sense that there was something I was supposed to learn from that young boy, but I didn't know what it was at that point in time. That answer I wouldn't discover until much later in life, but my gut instinct was correct.

CHAPTER FOUR

JAX, ALMOST 9

I didn't want to drop the rings, I had to keep them safe on their way down the aisle. I had spent two weeks practicing my duty with a throw pillow from our couch and my parents' wedding rings. The more I practiced the better I got. Mr. Charlie had told me I could balance them on my nose, but Mom wasn't having that. She shouted every single time I tried to walk in a straight line with them balanced - successfully I might add - on the tip of my nose. So back on the pillow they went. Anyway, I knew how important it was for the rings to make it down the aisle. They couldn't get married without them, so I was hyper focused on doing it right.

On the day of the wedding, we left extra early because of all the snow on the ground. I practiced in the backseat as the car slid through the streets of Kansas City with Dad quietly at the helm. I got to change clothes at the church because they wanted me to stay warm in case something happened with the car on the way there. Thankfully we made it safely and so did everyone else.

We all lined up in the back of the church while the guests entered through the doors of the sanctuary. I got to peek through the doors every now and then to take a look at who was out there. The church was full of mostly older adults, but there was a couple around my parents' age who had a daughter that looked my age. I was having trouble seeing her face because there seemed to be a light that reflected off of where she was walking and sitting. At first I wondered if she was an angel. I mean she was even wearing a white dress and everything, but I watched as her Mom held out a hand so she could spit out her gum and that's when I figured angels probably weren't gum chewers like humans were. I spent much of the rest of the time before the ceremony, trying to see past the light that shrouded her face. I didn't understand why I could see everyone else's face except for hers. I looked around at the others who were waiting and could see everything in great detail, down to the color of the frames they wore on their faces. Hers though felt out of focus because of the bright light that was just hovering nearby.

Suddenly I felt a tap on my shoulder and I stopped peeking through the doors. We were asked to get in line and I took one last deep breath with my mom before things got started. She walked in ahead of me and then the doors closed again. I remember looking up at Dr. Chris's Dad for the rings and he nodded at me and loosely tied them with the string on the pillow. They had Dr. Chris' niece lined up behind me with a basket of flower petals. I grabbed two from the bunch and stuffed them in my pocket. Then, as quickly as they had shut, the doors reopened and it was my turn to walk down the aisle with the rings perched atop of the pillow.

I stood beside Mr. Charlie at the front of the aisle and watched as Christina dropped the flower petals behind me. Then Corwin, Dr. Chris' nephew, came down the aisle ringing a bell and shouting to all that the bride was coming. I remember thinking how grateful I was that I wasn't asked to do that. When the doors opened again, everybody stood up and turned to watch Dr. Chris as she walked down the aisle, including the little girl whose face I couldn't see. I was busy trying to look around her parents to see if this angle was any different, but that dang light was still there! Frustrated, I was trying to figure out how I was going to see her face and then I heard sniffles. I looked up at Mr. Charlie, who was crying and smiling as he watched his bride walking down the aisle towards him. So sappy. I looked down the aisle at Dr. Chris and tried to understand what he was feeling. I didn't get it, until I did.

Dr. Chris' Dad handed off his daughter and I handed off the rings. We both took our seats in the pews. Then in the blink of an eye, I suddenly understood what Mr. Charlie was feeling.

There she was, at my Godfather's wedding, reciting a funny passage from The Princess Bride. Marley, the girl I sorta kinda cheated on Lola with the year before - but not really, was standing on a box in front of me, wearing a white dress with purple and red flowers on her wrist. She was the one I sent the peace dove to. It was her and now that I could finally see her face, she was so beautiful I lost control of all sense of what to do with my body. All my face wanted to do was smile, but I'd spent the last year perfecting how to be cool around all the girls. *"Steel yourself, Jax!"* played on an internal loop in my head all night long. I couldn't stop staring at her. I had wondered for a year if I'd ever get to meet the little girl with a boy's name who was "very grateful" for me, according to Dr. Chris.

This was my chance to meet her. But my face felt like it was having spasms. I wasn't supposed to be as impacted by her as I was, but I couldn't stop it - no matter how hard I tried. And man, did I try. My nearly 9 year old heart was completely overwhelmed with love and a sense that she was the girl I was going to spend my life with. That glowing light that shielded her face before now, surrounded her. I don't know if anyone else could see it, but I couldn't miss it.

I was so conflicted. I didn't want to look at someone the way Mr. Charlie looked at Dr. Chris. But how could I not look at her like that when I knew she was my person? When she finished reciting her lines from the movie, she talked about what it means to love each other - choosing each other every day, helping each other up when you fall, supporting and celebrating each other, not because you have to but because you choose to. The more she spoke, the brighter the light that surrounded her.

I wanted her to sit beside me after she finished reading. I even scooted over in my seat so there was room for her. My parents were both in the wedding party, so I was seated beside Dr. Chris' niece and nephew. She walked right by me on the way to her seat without even a glance in my direction. But when she passed by, there was a warmth that I felt in my soul. I didn't know what it was, but it was strong, and it contributed to the dance battle my face had with itself.

The wedding felt like it took too long. I was ready to get to the party so I could bump into Marley on the dance floor. But at every turn there were adults who were complimenting my bow tie and asking me to dance. I only wanted to dance with one person there and she would barely look at me.

During the first dance, everybody was busy looking at the bride and groom. I was looking at her, wondering how to get across the dance floor without interrupting the newlyweds. I looked at Mr. Charlie who just happened to catch my eye and smile. I returned the smile but quickly redirected my gaze towards the love of my life. I just had to figure out how to get closer to her. With their first dance officially complete, Mom and Dad, and other couples found their way out to the dance floor. I slowly began to meander my way around the room - moving from table to table so I could inch closer to Marley. Finally! With just one table between us, I stood up to make my move and was immediately greeted by a tap on the shoulder - I disliked that part about being little. Nobody called your name, they just stayed tapping me on my shoulder. Anyway, Mom tapped me on my shoulder and asked if she could dance with me. That was the only time I ever thought to deny my mother a dance. I was so close to her, Marley. She was right there, but so was my mom. So I took her out on the dance floor and kept a close eye on Marley during that mother and son dance.

"Do you go to school with Marley, son?" Mom asked me during our dance.

"Not that I know of Mom" I blurted out. I was afraid she was going to ask more questions that I didn't really have the answer to.

"You sure have been keeping an eye on her all day and night." Mom said as she looked down at me with a gaze of understanding.

"I have?"

"Now is not the time to play dumb, Jax. You know you have."

I laughed at the fact that Mom doesn't miss a single thing. "I have."

"Have you said hello yet?"

"No ma'am."

She spun me around in a circle as we continued to dance. "Well, let's go meet her and her family, buddy!"

"Mom! No!" I was mortified at the idea of meeting her with Mom in tow. She wasn't there at school when I was meeting different girls. Why did she want to meet Marley? And her family too? No way. I couldn't allow that to happen. I spun her around the dance floor and far away from Marley's table.

"Jax," she started as she danced me back in their general direction, "it doesn't have to be any major introduction. I'll be cool about it."

"No, Mom. You won't be. Remember when you found out that I broke my arm because I was trying to impress Lola. You weren't cool then."

"Jax, you didn't break your arm over Marley. But I'm sure her parents probably saw you staring at her too. We should probably go say hello."

The thought of her parents knowing that I was their daughter's future husband startled me back into staying cool. "Nah. I don't think they noticed. I'll just stop. It's okay."

The song ended and Mom curtsied in front of me as I took a bow and went to get some cake. By the time I made it back to our table they were passing out champagne flutes to everybody. Yes, even the kids. I couldn't believe they were letting us drink what the adults got to drink, but my glass looked exactly the same as Dad's glass - right down to the lump of coal that had sunk to the bottom of it. During the toast they called it a Sugarplum, but we were fresh off of Christmas and I just KNEW somebody had been bad and passed off all of the coal they'd received to the rest of us.

Anyway, I clinked glasses with everyone at the table. When Dad turned to toast with me, he said, "here's to old friends, AND NEW" and winked.

Even Dad was giving me a hard time. "Did you go say hi to your girlfriend yet, Jax?"

"I don't have a girlfriend anymore, Dad!" I told him matter of factly.

"Oh, sorry, I forgot about the Lola heartbreak."

I shook my head at my parents and just how bad they were about being subtle. We didn't know everybody at our table, but now they all knew my business and I was met with a chorus of sentimental mumbo jumbo.

"You're a cutie pie. You'll meet someone who won't break your heart soon enough."

"Don't you worry about one person. There are more fish in the sea, kiddo."

"Are you sure you're not the heartbreaker?"

"Oh you're young. You have plenty of time to find your person."

What they didn't know is that I'd found her already. Or she found me. I wasn't sure what was happening, but she was about to leave and I never made my way back near her table because I was taught to be respectful when adults were speaking to you - even if they were legit blocking your ability to meet one of those other fish in the sea that they were talking about. I was stuck - at the table - listening to all of their stories about heartbreak and how they met the loves of their lives while watching mine be handed a coat by her Dad. She was about to leave and I didn't get a chance to say hello because the adults in my life were being embarrassing as usual. I watched with deep sadness as her dad helped her put on her coat and escorted her to say goodbye to the bride and groom.

They passed by the table and I finally got to look her in the eyes. That warm feeling was back as soon as she was close by. I couldn't imagine a world where she wasn't in it. All I knew was this girl, that I didn't know, I was sent here to protect and to cherish; to love for all eternity. It felt like this life was a continuation of an eternal connection. I didn't have the words to explain it back then. But I do now. She was my person and I knew if I could find a way to meet her that she would understand it too.

Dr. Chris and Mr. Charlie were making the rounds to each table to thank everyone for facing the storms to share this day with them. When they got to our table, They both had questions. Lots of questions.

"So what'd you think of Marley buddy? I saw you trying to catch her eye all night."

"Charlie, leave him alone!" Dr. Chris laughed. "You know, if you want to meet her, we can set it up, right?"

I thought she was on my side. Turns out, I was wrong. This was clearly an every man for himself moment and I was out there - on a freakin' island.

"You know your Godfather is just playin, right Jax?" Mr. Charlie asked me.

"Yes, I know," I told him as he tussled my hair and thanked me for bringing the rings down the aisle. They both wished me Happy Birthday and handed me a present to be opened the next day. So when the countdown was finished at the end of the night, as everyone else was kissing their partner, I was opening my gift and thinking about my own - wondering if she was sleep or if she was awake, wondering how we were going to meet, and wondering how in the heck they knew I wanted this microscope for my birthday.

I didn't see the newlyweds again until they got back from their honeymoon about two weeks after their wedding. They came to Mom and Dad's house for dinner, as a married couple. Mr. Charlie was right. He didn't bring anyone over until he was sure he was going to marry them. If he could be that certain and trust what he was feeling in his gut, then I could too - even at 9 years old. I hugged them both when they came over and Dr. Chris stooped down and told me she had a special delivery for me. She handed me an envelope addressed to "The Ring Bearer." It was definitely written by a child and I hoped that it was written by her. I stuffed it in my back pocket and waited until after dinner to run up to my room and read it in peace.

"Dear Ring Bearer," it was clearly from a child who attended the wedding and I highly doubted that it came from Christina.

"My name is Marley," I was so excited that it was from her that I stopped reading and started staring at her handwriting. She wrote to me. I couldn't believe that she took the time to send me a message. I didn't think Dr. Chris was the type to trick me like this so it **HAD** to be real. I had a whole internal conversation about the fact that I was holding this letter from **HER** in my hands and then I realized that forgot to read the actual letter itself. So I went back to the beginning and started over.

"My name is Marley and I am 8 years old." *Okay we're around the same age.* **"I saw you staring at me during Dr. Chris' wedding."** *Oh no.* **"I am writing you to tell you that I like your smile."** *Okay, we in there, Jax!* **"Your face looks kind when you smile but not when you turn your smile off."** *Dang. I don't know how I feel about that.* **"You should leave it on more often. I like your kind face."** *Nope, we're good. She likes your face, Jax.* **"Did you have fun at the wedding?"** *I almost had fun at the wedding.* **"Please write me back."** *Yes! Here's your chance. She wants to talk to you.*

"Marley, (the girl who wore flowers on her wrist)" *I know exactly who you are and someday I'm gonna put some flowers on your wrist and a ring on your finger just like Mr. Charlie did with Dr. Chris.*

I pulled out a pencil but couldn't find a sharpener, so I found a purple marker instead. Then I couldn't find any paper anywhere, so I ran downstairs to ask for help. I had to write her back before Dr. Chris left tonight so she could deliver my letter.

I butted my way into their conversation, knowing this was more important than anything they were talking about. "Mom, I need a card or some paper!" I shouted as I flew down the stairs.

"Jax, your Godparents are about to become real parents to some children of their own!" Dad told me.

In my head I just thought that's what people did. They got married and then they had children. To me it was normal. It wasn't until later that I realized how infinitesimal the percentage is for actually conceiving and delivering healthy babies. "Yay! Congratulations! Does anybody have a card or some paper?"

Mom and Dad looked incredulous at my reaction. Dr. Chris had a bit more empathy.

"Oh, he'll get a chance to meet his God Siblings soon enough. Let's see if we can get this young man something to write on."

Mom looked like she trusted that Dr. Chris knew something she didn't and stood up to go grab a thank you card and envelope for me. "Will this do?" she asked me as she placed it in my hand.

"It's perfect! THANK YOU!" I shouted as I ran back upstairs to write a response to my beloved. I stopped midway up and turned around to look at Dr. Chris. "I'll be right back. Don't leave yet." She nodded in my direction.

I heard Mom ask what that was about and Dr. Chris responded. But I was too far upstairs to hear what she said.

I sat down at my desk and tried to write but nothing came out. I stretched across my bed. Still nothing. I went into child's pose on the floor and suddenly the words came flowing from my brain like lightning strikes in a thunderstorm. I knew I needed to hurry up and capture them before the storm passed.

Dear Marley,

Thank you for writing me. I had trouble seeing your face at the wedding because of the bright light that blocked your face. How could you see anything? It was so bright! When I finally got to see you I could not stop staring because you felt like a very good friend to me. That made me happy and sad. That is why my smile was turning on and off. But your letter turned my smile back on.

I almost had fun at the wedding but all the grown ups wanted to talk to me about love stuff when all I wanted to do was come say hi to you. I almost made it to your table but my Mom asked me to dance with her. I did not tell her this but I pretended she was you. You are the only person I ever want to dance with. I like you. I want to know more about you. I want to be friends with you. Do you want to be friends with me?

I liked what you said during your speech about how we can choose love. You chose to send me a letter and that feels like love to me.

How do you know Dr. Chris and Mr. Charlie? Write me back.

I love you Marley!
The Ring Bearer

In hindsight, I was more than a little overzealous. But we're talking about a newly 9 year old who was certain he was writing to his future wife. Of course he was going to be overzealous! I had no idea how I was going to make it work with her, but I trusted the universe to have my back. So I dropped in the two petals I'd snagged from Christina's basket, sealed the card in the envelope added my return address to the envelope like they taught us to do in school and confidently handed that thing over to Dr. Chris that evening. She tucked it away in her purse and told me that she'd deliver it to Marley as soon as she could.

Every time they came over, I asked if she'd seen Marley yet and for the first few months, she kept telling me that she wouldn't see her again for a few months. Then one day that May, Dad came in from checking the mail and Mom asked him what we got.

"Two bills, and an ad for the local supermarket," he said handing the mail to Mom. "Oh, and Jax got something," he said as he handed me the envelope. I tried to stay cool but Mom asked who sent me something. When Dad said, somebody named Marley my soul lit up like the light that surrounded Marley's face at the wedding. She'd received my card and sent me some mail!

"Who's Marley, Jax?" Mom asked, as she tried to grab the envelope from my hand.

I played keep away and told her that she was in Mr. Charlie's wedding.

"Oh, is that the little girl you were staring at? The one you didn't want to say hi to at the reception?" Dad asked me.

"Yes. She wrote me a letter after the wedding and I wrote her back. I thought she didn't want to be my friend but maybe she does if she wrote me back."

"What did your letter say, Jax? Why wouldn't she want to write you back?" Mom asked me.

"It said 'Do you want to be friends with me?'" I said, intentionally neglecting the fact that I'd told her that I love her and sent rose petals to her and carried on about how she felt like an old friend.

"I remember when you asked for that card," Dad remembered. "You were up there a mighty long time to just write one question. Is that all it said?" He asked me.

"There was more, but I need to go read this letter!" I was adamant.

"Read it right here, Jax!" Dad teased. Mom nodded her head in agreeance.

"Out loud?" I protested.

"No, you read it to yourself first. Then read it to us out loud," he joked.

I slowly opened the envelope, looking at Dad with spite, wondering why he was torturing me. I just wanted to hear from my love. I noticed there was a return address on this envelope, so I didn't have to wait for her to see Dr. Chris again so she could get my next letter.

I pulled the letter out of the envelope and one of the flower petals I had included in my letter fell out. There was a heart with the letter M drawn on it. It was too late to hide it.

Mom was on it, "Did she send you a flower, Jax? Who is this child?"

"Mom! This is one of the flower petals I sent to her. She sent it back!"

Dad picked it up off of my lap. "There's a heart on it, Sabrina."

Mom rubbed her forehead, "I can't believe we're here already, Steve. He's just 9!"

"When I was 9..."

Mom interrupted him, "What does the letter say, Jax? Read it out loud bud."

I sighed the biggest sigh I could muster up. That still didn't reverse the request from Mom. Instead, I now had to read the letter out loud the first time through, instead of reading it to myself first. I didn't know what Marley had written to me, but we were all about to find out - together.

Dear Ring Bearer,

You are welcome. Thank you for writing me back. Purple is my favorite color. How did you know?

I go to Crispus Attucks elementary school but school is almost over. Dr. Chris was my doctor when I got sick. She helped me to get better and kept me alive. I think I almost died or maybe I did for a little bit. But she fixed my brain and brought me back to life.

I could see just fine. There was not a light in my face at the wedding but there was a light behind you when you left your smile on. It was glowing. You felt like a good friend too even though I did not get to say hello. My parents thought we knew each other but I told them that I do not know you. I would like to be friends with you but I do not know your name. I think it's funny to call you ring bearer so I will keep calling you that if that is okay with you.

I like you, ring bearer. I want to know more about you. What do you want to know about me? I will tell you. What are you doing this summer? Please write me back.

I do love you ring bearer!

Your good friend,
Marley

p.s. Thank you for the rose petals. I sent one back. I hope it was not crushed when you got the letter. I will keep one and you keep one so we can remember each other.

I looked up at my parents when I finished reading the letter out loud. I had tears in my eyes. Mom had tears in hers, and when we looked at Dad - he was wiping some water from his eyes too.

"Would you like another card or some paper this time, Son?" Mom asked me as she stood up from her seat.

"I think we need to buy the boy some stationery, Sabrina," Dad said while nodding in my direction.

That was the start of our letter exchange, and it only got better from there.

ELEMENTARY SCHOOL LETTERS
- MARLEY & JAX -
AGE 9

Dear Marley,

Thank you for writing me back. I am glad that Dr. Chris was your doctor or else we could not write to each other. I am grateful that she fixed your brain. I am also grateful that you are alive and strong.

I like to be called Ring Bearer. Can I give you a nickname too? My Mom almost took me to your table after the wedding.

This summer I will get to go on vacation with my Mom and Dad but they are also making me read a lot of books. I get to choose the books I read though. I like reading about Raine the Brain. He seems super smart. I hope to be cool like him when I grow up and start middle school!

What are you doing this summer? What do you like to do for fun? What books do you like to read? Do your parents make you read during summer break too? I don't want to ask you too many questions. So I just have one more. Do you have a boyfriend? Okay, one more. Do you want one?

I love you Marley. Write me back!

Your good friend (and hopefully boyfriend),
The Ring Bearer

p.s. I like your handwriting. I will keep this rose petal forever.

Dear Ring Bearer,

You are welcome for the rose petal. I promise to keep mine for always too.

Do you like the paper that I am writing on? My Mom got this for me. She told me that every lady needs her own stayshunairy. I don't think I spelled that right but that is how it sounds. So anyway I guess I am a lady now which means you probably should just call me Marley.

I wish your Mom would have brought you to my table. What happened?

Where do you get to go on vacation? I love to read books! I have not heard of Raine the Brain but I will ask my librarian about those books. What else do you like to do? Do you play sports or video games? I like to write. I really like writing letters to this boy who would be my boyfriend if my Dad said I was old enough to have one. So he is just my really great friend who is also a boy until I can have one.

I am talking about you Ring Bearer.

You don't ask too many questions. What else do you want to know about me? Ask me and I will answer your questions.

I love you Ring Bearer! Please write me back.

Your great friend,
Marley

p.s. will you send me a postcard from your vacation?

Dear Lady Marley (hee hee hee),

Thank you for writing me back. The paper is pretty fancy. I am in South Dakota right now but we are on a road trip. We got to see the big heads made of rock that are on this postcard. They said some people carved them into the mountain. I am not sure why they would do that but they did. They call it Mount Rushmore but I think it took them a long time to make them.

How old do you have to be before you can have a boyfriend? I will wait for you.

I love you Marley. Write me back at my home.

Your best friend,
The Ring Bearer

Dear Ring Bearer,

Thank you for writing me back. I don't think we have to say that anymore. I will ALWAYS write you back.

Mount Rushmore looks kinda cool. My Dad said I can't have a boyfriend until I am 16. That feels like a long time. I will be twice as old as I am now by then. Doesn't that seem too old to date anybody?

Where else did you go on vacation?

I love you Ring Bearer. Please write me back.

Your bestest friend,
Marley

Dear Marley,

Now I am writing you on a new postcard from Minneapolis. We got to ride bikes on a trail and sail a boat on a lake. I love being outside and playing different sports. I think you asked me about that in a letter but I didn't have room on the last postcard to tell you my answer. Oh, and board games. I love board games. Do you play sports or video games or board games?

We will be home soon. I can't wait to read your letters.

I love you Marley! Remember to write me back at my home.

Your best friend,
The Ring Bearer

Dear Ring Bearer,

I love playing board games too! I don't think I am coordinated enough to play sports. When I fell in gym class they took me to the hospital and that's how they found my brain tumor. Maybe I am still afraid to try because they might find something else if I fall again. I will just cheer for you instead.

I hope you had fun on your vacation. I can't believe school is starting again soon. I hope I don't get chased home by that stupid doberman anymore. Dogs scare me so much!

How many books did you read this summer?

I love you Ring Bearer! Please write me back.

Your bestest bud,
Marley

Dear Marley,

We are back home now and I got to read two letters from you at one time!

Yes. Sixteen year olds are pretty much adults. That is way too old to start dating. You should already be engaged by then! I will wait for you though. Even if that means we'll be two old people before we can start dating. I will just be old with you.

I am glad that you fell so they could find what was wrong and fix it. Being afraid makes sense. It is also easy to be scared. You are a fighter Marley. You are the strongest kid I know. If they find something else you can fight that too and I promise I will be there to help you because we are best friends now. We will cheer for each other.

Summer break was not long enough for me. I read 10 books this summer. How many did you read? How many did you write?

I love you Marley! Write me back.

The Ring Bearer

p.s. Will we need to use a cane when we are 16?

MIDDLE SCHOOL LETTERS
- MARLEY & JAX -
AGE 12

Hey there, Ring Bearer!

OMG, can you believe we've been writing each other since we were 8 years old? That's like forever and a day! Middle school is so weird, and that stupid dog STILL chases me home every day, but it's awesome having you to share the awkwardness with.

You asked me about the weirdest teachers at my school in your last letter. Well, there's Mr. Johnson and his crazy hair. It's like he's trying to compete with a tornado or something! And don't even get me started on Mrs. Thompson's "fun" math quizzes. I swear she's secretly a math genius from another planet!

Anyway, how's your new school year going? Are there any cute classmates there? Just kidding... sort of. Let me know all the juicy details!

Can't wait to hear back from you. Please write me back.

I love you.

Your BFF,
Marley

Hi Marley!

I got your letter!

Yep, I totally agree with you. Middle school is a roller coaster of craziness! Mr. Johnson's hair must be a secret alien experiment gone wrong. And Mrs. Thompson? She's probably plotting to take over the world. I wish I could walk you home and protect you from that dog. Maybe one day when we're married we'll get a dog you like...jk - unless you want one "fur"real (lol).

Anyway, my new school year is okay, I guess. 6th grade feels different. Like I'm older but I'm not old enough for grownups to trust me. There might be a cute classmate or two, but none of them compare to my awesome best friend. I can't wait until we're 16 and I can take you out on a date. I'll be sure to bring you a cane. Remember when I thought that was old?

BTW, did you see the new superhero movie? I know you're a superhero geek like me! Do you think your Dad would be okay with a superhero movie marathon? Just two friends hanging out I mean...

Write me back.

Love you loads,
Ring Bearer

Hiya Ring Bearer!

OMG, seriously! I think Mrs. Thompson might secretly enjoy torturing us with those quizzes.

I do remember when we thought 16 year olds were supposed to be married. Now that it doesn't feel so far away I think that's too young to be engaged. LOL

So, about that superhero movie marathon...I got grounded for not cleaning my room. It was like a superhero disaster zone in there! But hey, you know what they say, "With great messiness comes great consequences."

And guess what? I joined the school's drama club! I know, I know, it's not exactly superhero stuff, but it's fun! I promise I won't turn into a drama queen though.

I love you. Please write me back...

Your Future First Date,
Marley

p.s. I won't keep you from getting a dog, but I guess that means we're not getting married. LOL

Hey Marley!

Our first date can't get here soon enough. I think the first thing I want to do when I see you is give you a big hug. Then can we dance together? I spend a lot of time thinking about how much I wanted to dance with you at that wedding. Do you even like to dance? I never asked.

Drama club sounds super cool! Break a leg (but not literally, that would be bad). I bet you'll rock it, and maybe one day you'll play a superhero in a play!

My school has this weird cafeteria food. I think they invented a new food group. I call it, "Mystery Meat Surprise." I'm pretty sure the lunch ladies are secretly evil scientists testing their concoctions on us. Is the meat weird at your school too?

Oh, and speaking of superheroes, did I tell you about the new comic book I found? It's called "The Adventures of Awkwardman and Shygirl." Totally reminded me of us, except we're way cooler!

Stay awesome and don't let the dog send you running. The right one will love you just like I do.

I love you, Shygirl - Marley Mar!

Write me back!

Your friendly neighborhood pal,
Ring Bearer

Hi Ring Bearer,

Haha, "Mystery Meat Surprise"? More like "Mystery Meat Disaster" and I avoid it at all costs. They do have some really good cookies though and I usually eat those for lunch.

I have to tell you a secret, I'm kind of a terrible dancer but that doesn't stop me from dancing. I just let my limbs do what they feel like doing and most of the time they find the rhythm. Most of the time. But I'll dance with you as long as that wouldn't embarrass you.

"The Adventures of Awkwardman and Shygirl"? That's epic! We could have our own comic series! We'd fight awkwardness and spread friendship all over the world!

You're the true superhero in my life, and I'm so lucky to have you! Please write me back.

Love you lots!

Your Forever Fan,
Marley

p.s. We'll see about the dog. They terrify me!!

Dear Marley Mar,

It doesn't matter how you dance. I've never seen a superhero dance on beat either. If it helps, I'll dance off beat too. You're the only person I ever want to dance with.

We just had our spring dance and I went with my friends. All the guys stood together and all the girls stood on the other side of the gym. That's when I wished you were there. I would've met you in the middle of the floor so we could superhero dance together. Awkwardman and Shygirl, taking over the dance floor and and bringing joy to middle school dances everywhere. Sounds like an epic adventure to me.

I love you for eternity, in this world and all the others that exist.

Write me back!
Ring Bearer

p.s. I'm sending one of my school pictures so you can see what I look like now. Send me one of yours? I want to draw the cover for our comic book and we can write the first story together. Is that okay with you?

My Ring Bearer!

You're even more cute now than I remember from the wedding. How come you didn't date anyone this year? Sheesh!

I put a picture of me in the envelope. Eeeek!

I can't believe this school year is over. I can't wait to create a comic book adventure with you. Are we starting with the school dance like you mentioned in your last letter? This is going to be so cool!

I love you a whole lotta. Please write me back.

The girl from the wedding,
Marley

p.s. My Mom and Dad just caught me staring at your picture and both of them thought it was so cute that I have a crush on my pen pal. I don't think they know what we know yet. But they'll find out when we're 16, right?

My Marley!

You just keep getting cuter and cuter. I like your glasses! There's no other person out there for me. Why waste their time and mine?

My parents just saw me staring at your picture too. They make me read the letters to them every now and then. This was one of those times. I was just staring into the envelope, looking at your face and Mom asked me what was wrong. When I showed her the picture she said you were a cutie pie.

You're right. I don't think they get it. But we do and that's all that matters Shygirl. Maybe we should write that into one of our comic book stories. Oh, I put a copy of the cover and some story ideas in the envelope with this letter. Whaddaya think? We can create a Google Doc to work on it together if your parents are okay with it.

I love you, Marley Mar.

Write me back!
Ring Bearer

p.s. I know it's still a few years away, but what do you wanna do on our first date? I wanna make sure I plan something you'd like.

CHAPTER FIVE
MARLEY & JAX,
AGE 16

Marley:

One Friday evening in September, I was getting mentally prepared to go babysit the twins and Vonnie for Dr. Chris and Charlie again. It wasn't bad once they were older, but three young children were a handful for grownups so you can imagine what it was like for 16 year-old me. As long as they didn't realize that they outnumbered me I knew I'd be fine. They were all as intelligent as they come, so I was just biding my time really.

Dad checked the mail when he got home from work and as he slumped his way into the house, he tossed a letter in my direction. "You and the Ring Bearer still writing each other, baby girl?"

"We are, Dad." I told him after thanking him for the

mail.

I always waited to open his letters. There was something about reading them first thing in the morning that always helped me start the day off on the right foot. This letter was different though. I opened it right away to see what the Ring Bearer had to say about taking so long to write me back this time. I hadn't received a letter from him since I transferred into my new high school.

Marley,

I'm sorry for taking so long to write. We went from writing each other once a week, to once a month, and now I've taken several months to respond to your last letter. It doesn't have anything to do with you. I still love you like the first day I saw you. I need some advice from my good friend though.

There's someone new at my school and I think I like her - a lot. But I want her to get to know me, the real me, the version of me that you know, not the version of me that she sees in high school. I'm not sure how to do that without looking like the weirdo that I actually am.

How has your new school been treating you? Have you made any new friends yet?

Write me back.

I love you, Marley!
The Ring Bearer

I looked at the clock to see if I had time to write a response. If I kept it short I could still be there on time so I pulled out my pen and the stationery that Mom bought me the summer before we lost her. I'd written so many letters to The Ring Bearer since that year that my supply was running low, which very much felt like I was losing my mother all over again. I tucked that feeling away inside myself and instead gave the Ring Bearer the best response I could generate in ten minutes time.

Ring Bearer,

Sometimes I wonder how you could be anything different than who you are in your letters. Which version of you feels the most genuine? You should be that person whenever you can be. You'll attract the people who love you as you are - even when you take an unusually long time to write them back and then only write back when you want help.

If you like this person, you should find a way to spend time with her. Listen to her. Really listen to her.

The new school is...interesting. There's a guy who stares at me when I walk down the hallways and when his friends laugh at him for doing it, he resorts to insulting me. I don't even know him, but he's a tall drink of cyanide. Looks good on the outside, but definitely not good for my soul. Sometimes I don't want to go to school because I just know that Jackson is going to be a jerk to me. But I go anyway, because one bad act won't stop the show. Plus, Dad enrolled me in this school to challenge me academically. So I'm doing my best to focus on going to school to actually learn something instead of treating it like the cesspool social experiment that it feels like.

Anyway, that's all I have for now. I've missed your letters good friend. Tell me what's new. Please write me back.

Love you lots,
Marley

I set the letter aside because it took me way longer than 10 minutes to write and I still wanted to make sure that I was on time at the Hughes' residence. I reminded Dad where I was going and told him where I stored his dinner for the evening, then off I went to my car - really it was Mom's old car, so I could drive 15 minutes across town to babysit for the evening.

I hugged Dr. Chris and Mr. Charlie when I got there and they introduced me to their friend Janae and her fiancé, Evan. The four of them were going to hang out that evening, which is why they needed the babysitter. What they didn't tell me until I got there is that I would also be babysitting Janae's daughter, who was also about the same age as the twins.

"But," they told me, "we brought in some help. He's on the way and should be here soon."

There was a knock at the door just as they finished that thought. Mr. Charlie opened it and there he was - Jackson. The same jerk I had just written about in my letter.

"Oh, I don't think I'll need any help," I told them.

"Well I'm already here for the night, so let's figure out how to make this work," he said while staring at me the same way his friends made fun of him for doing at school.

"The two of you got it from here right?" Dr. Chris said as she patted Jackson on the back while walking past him on her way out the door.

"Jackson, lock the door behind us," Mr. Charlie told him.

We stared at each other for a solid 30 seconds without saying a word. I finally asked him if he could watch all four kids while I got dinner started.

He smirked at me, "I think I can handle that. If you need something, just holler and I'll come help you."

"Oh, yeah, okay," I mumbled on my way into the Hughes' newly remodeled kitchen.

"How much time do you think it will take to make dinner? I want to make sure we're ready when you are, so you don't have to wait on us to get it together."

Who was this guy? I was fairly certain that he was not the Jackson that I went to school with. Maybe he had a cousin with the same first name. "Can you give me about 35 minutes? That way I can fix dinner and get the table set."

"We'll set the table, Marley," he said as he fought back a smile and headed towards the playroom where all four children, three 5-year olds and an almost 3-year old, were hanging out watching tv.

I heard them holler his name with such excitement when he knocked on the door. I knew then that there must have been something good in him or they definitely would've had a different reaction.

Just like cyanide, I repeated to myself. *Looks like water. Tastes like death.*

In 30 minutes, the meal I had made for them was ready to be transferred to the table that I forgot to set. I peeked in the dining room after hearing little feet running around in there. They were following Jackson's lead, setting the table. First their plates, then their cups, then silverware and napkins. "Okay, I'm going to help her bring the food to the table. Y'all wait quietly right here. Will you do that for me?"

"Yes!" they emphatically replied at once.

I rushed back into the kitchen as stealthily as I could.

"I'll be right back," I heard him share as his voice appeared to get closer. I turned around when I heard a thud near the edge of the kitchen and found him leaning on the doorframe, staring at me again but smiling this time.

I didn't say a word out loud, but I did have to repeat my mantra over and over again as he slowly walked in my direction. *Looks like water. Tastes like death. Looks like water. Tastes like death. Looks like water...*suddenly his arm stretched around me as he reached for the bowl of bread. I held my breath...*Tastes like death. Smells like heaven.*

I turned around to face him and his eyes softened as he deepened his stare. "What else can I grab, Marley?" he said softly before realizing how the words sounded as they exited his mouth. His body straightened up as stiff as a board. It looked like someone had popped him with a rubber band, "I mean, the food, what other food can I move to the table, Sweetheart? Marley. Sorry, I'll just take this bread in and I'll be right back."

Mantra on repeat. *Looks like water. Tastes like death. Looks like water. Tastes like death. Looks like water. Tastes like death.*

Jax:
When they called me earlier in the week to see if I could help Marley babysit, I knew that I'd rearrange whatever I had to so I could be there. They knew that we were still exchanging letters with each other. They knew that she didn't know who I was yet and I hoped that Friday night wouldn't give too much away. I knew I was going to tell her soon. I just didn't know how. I guess maybe I hoped that she would just instinctively feel it that night.

I'd been stalling on writing her back since she transferred into the same high school as me. I was a different person in my letters to her than I was at school. Over the last 8 years or so I had matured into this nerves of steel cool kid who couldn't be bothered with any of the bureaucracy of high school. Jackson was a facade. Inside I was still Jax, the little boy who wanted to be friends with everybody, who desperately loved his best friend and pen pal, Marley, who he now got to see every day. I didn't want her to see the version of me who made fun of her when his friends were being jerks, but I knew that showing her the real me, meant I'd have to blow up Jackson, the persona. But the more I got to see her in person, the more I felt like

Jackson had to go.

I wrote her back and mailed the letter on Tuesday, hoping it would reach her before she came to babysit on Friday. I hoped that it would just click. That she would know it was me and we could get married already. But Dad told me to trust the process, and so did Mr. Charlie. So I did. But that dang process was taking a very long time.

I played games with the kids on that Friday night while she was in the kitchen cooking something that smelled amazing. It very much felt like what I imagined our married nights would be like. Except in that moment, I was the guy from school that she hated. I made it my goal to let her see the real me that night. So I asked my God Brothers and God Sister for help, and Ms. Janae's daughter asked if she could help too. They helped me set the table and sat like little angels in the dining room while I went to help Marley move the food in so we could eat. I bumbled through the first ask and ended up sounding like a perv. I walked out of the kitchen shaking my head. The kids took one look at me and in their loudest kid whispers asked how it was going. I shushed them, placed the bread on the table and said I'd be right back. I took one deep breath and turned around, ready to receive more food from Marley.

This time I knocked on the doorframe and asked how I could help. She stared into my eyes and handed me a bowl of Chicken Alfredo pasta, no words exited her mouth. It even looked like she was holding her breath. I made her nervous, which is not at all what I wanted.

I smiled at her, "You made all of this in 30 minutes?"

She nodded, grabbed the bowl of fruit salad, finally exhaled, and followed me out of the kitchen.

"Marlo, would you say grace for us?" she asked the

oldest of the twins. There we were at the heads of the table, eating dinner with 4 kids, managing things like it was nothing. Then things got interesting.

"Marley, did I see some Sugarplums in the kitchen?" I asked her. All four children erupted in cheers.

"Jackson, those are Dr. Chris' Sugarplums. I'm not sure we should give them to the kids without asking first."

The insult flew out of my mouth like a dagger before I even realized it was on the way. "You four eyed square." I was just so used to doing it at school that it was a reflex.

All the kids gasped and looked at me. I looked at Marley and the tears that were quickly welling up in her eyes. I was embarrassed. I had embarrassed her. Then the littlest one of the bunch pointed her finger at me and demanded that I "**POLOGIZE!**"

Marley and I were in a stare down. "**POLOGIZE NOW!!!**" Vonnie screamed at me.

Marley addressed my assailant, "Vonnie, nobody owes me an apology. Especially if he did it on purpose."

"It wasn't on purpose," I said softly. Marley didn't blink. The other children got rowdy. I cleared my voice and spoke louder, "I'm sorry for insulting you, Marley. I apologize for even thinking it and especially for letting it escape my mouth." The children turned their heads in Marley's direction, like they were watching a table tennis match.

"...and?" She waited. Their heads whipped back in my direction.

"And what?" I asked. Back towards Marley they looked.

"An apology also includes what you'll do differently in the future." The ball was in my court so to speak. All eyes were on me.

"YEAH!!!" Vonnie declared drawing the attention away

from me for a split second.

They looked back at me, "...and I'll think about how damaging my words can be before I let them out of my mouth instead of after."

"So you're still going to insult me. You're just going to think about how hurtful it'll be first?"

"No. I meant." I took a deep breath and slowed down my thinking. "I'll be more considerate of how harmful my words can be and hopefully that will minimize my chances of insulting you in the future. That's not at all how I feel about you."

Their little heads whipped so hard towards Marley, that I thought they were going to fall over in their chairs. She didn't say anything at first. She just stared at me like she was trying to sift through my bull.

"I promise I'm not who you see at school, Marley."

"Why do you stare at me so much, Jackson?"

"He loves you!" Vonnie blurted out before covering her mouth. She was too excited to spill the beans.

"Isn't it about your bedtime, Vonnie?" I asked.

"No! No! No!" she shouted.

"I think it must be close."

"No it's not brother!" she said. The 5 year olds all looked down at their empty plates at the same time.

Marley's eyes glared in my direction, "Jackson, meet me in the kitchen please."

Marley:

"Why would Vonnie say that, Jackson? What's going on?" He inched closer to me with each response.

"I have a crush on you, Marley. That's why."

"That's why what?" I asked him.

Closer still. "That's why she said it. That's why I stare at you so much. That's why I give you such a hard time and now that I've said that out loud it seems stupid to make fun of someone that you like so I'll stop doing it."

He was standing right in front of me with apologetic eyes. "Just give me tonight to show you, Marley." He reached out and held my hand. "Hey…"

I blinked out of my trance of confusion and looked down at my hand, resting in Jackson's.

"Hey…" he repeated again. "Marley, breathe." I didn't know I had been holding my breath until he said something. Then I gasped down as much air as my lungs could gobble up. He was still standing there, not making fun of me for not breathing. Nodding at me as if to let me know that I was safe. *Looks like water. Tastes like death. Looks like water. Tastes like death.*

"Jackson…I'm not sure what's happening right now."

He smiled at me, then quickly suppressed it. "What's happening is that the truth is finally being revealed."

Before he could continue, Chuck walked into the kitchen to check on me. He held my other hand and looked up at me, asking if I was okay. He had such a gentle spirit, like his Dad.

I told him I was okay and asked if he could get everyone to bring their plate into the kitchen for me. He nodded at me, then glared at Jackson as he walked back to the dining room. I let go of both of their hands at the same time and discovered that Jackson looked like he was still waiting to finish his thought. "Hey, can we just talk about this after we get them to bed?" I asked him.

"We can talk about it whenever you're comfortable, Marley. I'm not going anywhere, except to put a movie on so I can wash the dishes really quickly while the rest of you hang out."

He started filling the sink with water and dish soap and thanked each of the kids by name as they brought in their plate and glass. I collected their forks and was going to throw away their paper napkins, but Jackson grabbed them from my hand on his way back from the playroom where he'd already turned on the live animated version of Lady and the Tramp. How poetically apropos with our situation.

He tossed the napkins in the trash and added the silverware to the bubbly water in the sink. I attempted to return to the kitchen to do the work, and he gently turned me around and ushered me back to the playroom - his hand resting at the small of my back the entire way there. I could feel it lingering there through the start of the movie even though he was in another room on the opposite side of the house. The children were quiet as they watched the movie. Chuck and Vonnie both snuggled up near me, Vonnie on my lap and Chuck immediately to my right. Marlo and Chris hung out together on the floor, trading jokes of their own.

A lanky figure entered the doorframe and I turned my head to find Jackson, smiling at the 5 of us. I wondered what he was thinking in that moment, but I didn't stop to ask.

"Can I sit beside you?" He asked me. I confirmed with a head nod. Chuck glared at him for a split second and in the blink of an eye he was back to gushing over the movie.

Vonnie fell asleep on me and I asked Jackson if he would watch the rest of them while I put her to bed. While she was still asleep, I put her in her pjs and tucked her into bed, turning on the baby monitor so I could hear if she woke up. When I returned downstairs, I snuck a peek in the kitchen. It was spotless and I was impressed. Back in the playroom, Chuck had scooted over into the spot where I was sitting. I asked him if I could sit in his old spot on the floor and he nodded. He watched the movie for about 15 more minutes before he got up and sat on my lap and nuzzled in for some pre-sleep cuddles.

He was significantly heavier than his baby sister and there wasn't a couch to rest my back against where I was sitting. Jackson could tell I was uncomfortable. He lightly squeezed my shoulder and motioned for me to use his as a backrest. I tried it, but I just couldn't get comfortable. Then he slid his arm around me and I nuzzled in the same way that Chuck had done with me. I was a perfect fit in his arms, but I kept waiting for him to poke me or whisper mean somethings in my ear. Not even 5 minutes after I got comfortable, Chuck felt even heavier than normal in my arms. That's when I looked down and realized that he had fallen asleep too.

"Pass him to me," Jackson leaned down and whispered in my ear. I nodded and whispered goodnight to Chuck who sleepily hugged me before allowing himself to be carried out by Jackson. I heard him singing on the monitor in the boys' room that must've been on the same channel as Vonnie's room.

"You are my sunshine, my only sunshine."

Chuck sang back to him, "You make me happy, when skies are gray."

Then together, "You'll never know dude, how much I

love you. Please don't take my sunshine away."

This was NOT the same Jackson that I knew from school.

Once Chuck was sufficiently sleep, Jackson came back into the playroom where the other two were still giggling over the movie and I had shifted to a more comfortable position on the floor.

Jax:

When I got back from taking Chuck to bed, she had moved to another spot on the floor and was smiling at me as I entered the room. She waved the baby monitor at me.

I sat down beside her, "Oh, you heard that huh?" I tried to whisper before being shushed by Marlo and Chris. "Y'all shushing people now?" I joked with them and they giggled.

The two of them looked like best friends hangin out on the floor and I was a bit jealous that I couldn't hang with Marley like that. She was my best friend, but she didn't know that she was because I was too afraid to tell her that I was The Ring Bearer. Instead, we sat on the floor beside each other watching the movie. I didn't have a reason to put an arm around her for support anymore, so I just sat close by. She scooted over until our shoulders touched and quietly hummed the same song I had just been caught singing with Chuck. I smiled in her direction and stared in her eyes. That same warmth that I'd felt at the wedding and reception was suddenly back and it took my breath away.

"Jackson," she quietly called as I got lost in her eyes.

"Jackson, breathe."

I nodded quickly as a single tear fell from my left eye. "Are you okay?" She asked me, wiping my cheek dry just as fast as the tear dropped.

"Yeah, I think I just,"

She softly interjected out of concern, "Are you sure, Jackson? Your pupils are dilated!"

I tried to look away, but I couldn't. "Yours are too, Marley."

"Oh!" She turned her attention towards the last two that were in the room with us. "I think we lost them too," she whispered as she looked at their overlapping bodies as they appeared to try to comfort each other to sleep.

I saw them on the floor, but I couldn't keep my eyes off of her. It was just like the wedding all over again.

"Which one do you want to carry?" She asked me.

I didn't say anything, just continued to gaze at Marley and wondered if she knew yet.

"Jackson?" She asked, turning her head back in my direction. "Which one..."

This time I did the interrupting. "Can I kiss you?" A lonely tear ran from my left eye as my heart raced while I waited for her answer. Three heavy breaths exited her mouth.

"Which one do you want to carry to bed?"

"I'll carry the boy child. Meet me in the hallway when you've put Chris to bed in Vonnie's room?"

She nodded gingerly, almost as if she were uncertain if she trusted me enough to do that.

I put Marlo to bed and sang to him the same way I had to his brother. Before I left the room, he whispered one final word of encouragement to me, "Be kind to her."

I met Marley in the hallway at nearly the same time.

We closed the doors and our eyes locked again. I asked if she still had the baby monitor for Vonnie's room. She held it up.

"Follow me?"

I took her outside to the back patio and sat in the glider with her. We started on opposite ends of it as she looked up into the night sky and I spent my time gazing at her.

I apologized for asking if I could kiss her and for every time that I made fun of her at school. It was just a word salad that came flowing out of my mouth. She reached out and held my hand without turning in my direction.

"Why are you so mean to me Jackson? Tonight you were a different person. I actually like this version of you. Don't you think others would too?"

"I think they'd probably call me soft and make fun of me."

"How much is it worth for you to be yourself?"

She had rendered me silent.

"When you asked if you could kiss me, I wanted to say yes. But the Jackson I met tonight could be different from the Jackson that I'll see at school on Monday. I honestly couldn't risk that for myself. Say we kiss, and I fall head over heels in love with you, but come Monday, you treat me like crap again. I've set myself up for disappointment."

"I don't think I can go back to treating you like that after actually spending time with you, Marley. It's exactly as I imagined it would be."

"What do you mean like you imagined?"

"That's what I was thinking about when I was so busy staring at you all those times, even tonight. Promise me that you'll be open minded about what I'm about to say,

Marley."

"Sure, Jackson."

"Marley, there's a warm feeling in my soul when I'm near you."

"Me too, Jackson."

"I need you to know something, Marley."

"What do you want to marry me or something?" she asked jokingly.

I tilted my head and stared deep into her soul as the glider rocked us through the night.

"Jackson."

"Can I take you out on a date sometime, Marley? Let me earn it. I'll be kind to you at school and when you're ready, when you trust me, say yes to a date with me."

She bobbed her head. "Do you promise to keep asking me?"

"I promise, Marley. I won't stop unless you ask me to."

I jumped as Mr. Charlie nearly shouted from behind me, "You won't what, Jax?!"

"Oh, it's not what you think, sir. I promise," I told him. Dr. Chris was standing beside him rubbing his shoulder in what looked like an attempt to calm him down.

"Are you okay, Marley?" He asked her directly.

"I'm fine Mr. Charlie. It really isn't what it sounded like. All of the kiddos are in bed and we've been out here talking about why Jackson is so mean to me at school and so different here."

I dipped my head in shame. I don't know that my Godparents ever knew me as mean. I could feel a lecture coming on.

I stood to my feet, "Can I walk her to her car before you tear me a new one?"

Mr. Charlie, shooed us on as we handed him the baby

monitor. I could see how frustrated he was with me. I walked Marley to her car and hugged her goodbye for the evening, whispering one more apology in her ear for being such a jerk to her at school.

Her hug felt like home, and I was even more lost than I was before that night. I was more certain she was my wife than ever before. Even when she was mad at me, her light was still bright. I just wanted to stay cuddled up with her while Chuck was asleep on her lap. It felt so natural, like that was how we'd be as grown ups. In that moment I knew I wanted to marry that girl. I couldn't imagine my life without her as my friend, but if we could somehow merge the two, friendship and whatever the vibe was that was so clear between us, we would be unstoppable.

Marley:
I got home that night and checked on Dad. He had eaten dinner and was already sleep on the couch. I left him a note that I'd made it home safely so he could continue to rest. He hadn't been getting much sleep since Mom passed. So anything I could do to contribute to that the better for his sake.

I went upstairs to my room as quietly as possible. Man I was so grateful I didn't have time to mail that letter to The Ring Bearer earlier. I had a lot more to add.

p.s. I just got back from babysitting some children and guess who was there. Yep, the mean jerk that I just wrote about above. But guess what! I don't think he's actually as mean as he acts at school. I think he really likes me, Ring Bearer. He kept finding reasons to get close to me and at one point he asked if he could kiss me - as a tear fell from his eye. And. I. Wanted. To. Kiss. Him. So. Badly. But I didn't want him to think that being mean to me was okay. So he asked me on a date, but he told me not to say yes until I trusted him. So, yes. Be yourself around the girl that you like. I promise she's probably waiting for a good guy like you. Heck, if we were in the same school I bet things would be different.

p.p.s. Show her your light. I know how you sometimes stop yourself from smiling. Is that just a guy thing? Jackson did the same thing tonight! If you feel like smiling at her, smile at her. Be yourself and I promise she'll love you as much as I do.

p.p.p.s. Don't forget to send me an invitation to your wedding to new girl - wait, what's her name? Oh never mind. I still call you Ring Bearer. What's the difference? I'll keep an eye on my mailbox for an invitation that New Girl and Ring Bearer invite me to share in the joy of their nuptials.

p.p.p.p.s. I think I'm sleepy. Goodnight, Ring Bearer.

HIGH SCHOOL LETTERS
- MARLEY & JAX -
AGE 16

Dear Marley,

Good morning!

You wait to read my letters first thing in the morning? That's so sweet.

This Jackson guy sounds like a real piece of work. I can't believe he actually asked to kiss you. Don't give him too much slack. Make him work really hard for it. If he really likes you, he'll find a way to do better.

I feel like we're living parallel lives right now. You're the new girl getting picked on by a guy you described as cyanide, which I guess makes him toxic? I'm the toxic guy with a crush on the new girl. I've been taking your advice though. I don't want to be the toxic guy anymore, so I'm focusing on being myself.

Thank you for being you. I love you more than you know. Write me back.

The Ring Bearer

Dear Ring Bearer,

Why are you so different in person than you are in your letters? Are you afraid that people will find out that you're kind at heart? I sometimes look at Jackson and wonder why he can't be more like you.

Sometimes he does and says things that remind me a lot of you. But in the back of my mind I'll always remember how he first treated me and I don't think I can forget that. I want to. I'm trying to. But so far, I can't help but think about how crappy he treated me.

He keeps asking me out like he promised me he'd do when we were babysitting. I feel like it's a waste of his time and energy though. There are girls all over the school that I'm sure would love to go on a date with him. Should I tell him to stop?

We just got paired together for a group project in science class and I'm feeling some kinda way about it. PLEASE tell me you're having better luck with the new girl than I'm having over here.

Please write me back.

Love you lots!
Marley

Good Morning Marley,

I'm not making much ground with the new girl. I think she likes me, but probably like you and that Jackson dude, she doesn't trust that this version of me is the real me. I understand it. I don't like it, but I understand it.

I hope Jackson knows how lucky he is to be paired with the smartest girl I know. If you were my partner I'd ask lots of questions. I'd find a way to tell a lot of corny science jokes. I'd probably even ask to borrow your notes all so I could be closer to you.

Maybe don't tell him to stop, but definitely keep an eye on him.

Write me back.

I love you to the moon and back!
The Ring Bearer

Dear Ring Bearer,

Are you psychic?

He did all of those things! Every single one of them. But I think it's working. He's really funny and I think I'm starting to trust him - at least a little bit. The next time he asks me out, I'll probably tell him yes.

What's new with you? Please write me back.

Love you lots,
Marley

Good Morning, Marley,

What's new with me? I'm jealous. He better treat you right. That's all I have to say.

I've wanted to ask you out for a long time, but we weren't old enough to start dating until now. I know you're about to go out with Jackson, but promise me you'll let ME take you to prom. I joke a lot, but I'm serious. I know we haven't seen each other since we were 8, but I'd love to be your date.

Yes, I'm trying to ask you before Jackson does. Don't hate me. Write me back.

I love you,
The Ring Bearer

Ring Bearer,

I missed school last week and I borrowed Jackson's notes from Science class. You two have the same handwriting. Not similar. The same.

Are you him? Are you related to him? What's happening?

Please write me back.

Love you lots,
Marley

Good Morning Marley,

Short answer. Yes.

There's so much more for me to tell you.
Call me. Please.

I love you,
JW
The Ring Bearer

Good Morning Marley,

I know why you're not speaking to me. I deserve it. But you deserve the whole truth.

You are a fighter. Remember you're strong even when you don't feel like it.

Please answer my calls or write me back. You said you'd always write me back. I'll try to be more patient.

Happy Thanksgiving.

I love you, always.
Jax

Jackson, Jax, Ring Bearer - I'm not sure what to call you now,

Happy New Year and Happy Birthday.

I'm sorry it's taken me so long to write back. I was confused. I was hurt. I was embarrassed, and that last letter was on the last piece of stationery that my Mom had given me before she died.

I had a meltdown. Dad told me to give myself some space. So that's what I did.

You called me a lot and I didn't answer any of your calls. I was trying to figure out what to do. I couldn't put words to what I was feeling. Until now...

You could have told me who you were when you saw me at school. I felt manipulated and lied to. I thought you were a different person than you are. I felt foolish for believing that you loved me. Love is holding each other through grief and walking beside each other in joy. You've done both of those already.

Love is supporting each other's dreams and never allowing doubt to creep in. You definitely support my dreams, but there was so much doubt. And it didn't just creep in. It washed in like a flood.

Love is unspoken tenderness that adds light and life to others with each passing hour. But those insults didn't add light or life as they came from your mouth like daggers. In fact, they did the opposite.

Love is communicating why you're angry and coming to a resolution together, which is why I'm writing you. I love you and I can't keep these thoughts to myself. We're supposed to figure it out together. So here's what I need to know from you and I need the truth. Why wouldn't you tell me? Why were you so mean to me? How do you really feel about me?

Write me back.

Love you lots,
Marley

Marley,

Good morning! Thank you for writing me back.

I was scared. I still am. I'm afraid of so much. The girl of my dreams went from only existing in my mind, to being right in front of my face. I couldn't help but stare because you're more beautiful in person than I had built up in my imagination and you were real. Then I thought about how little the other kids at school knew me.

You're the one who knows me better than I know myself. You're the one who encouraged me to be myself so I could attract the new girl - who was you. But you didn't know it. You loved me enough to help me get whatever I wanted - even if you thought it was someone else.

I was going to tell you it was me when we were babysitting, but my God Brothers and God Sister kept us busy. Just so you know, Mr. Charlie and Dr. Chris, they know we exchange letters. They knew that night, that I hadn't told you I was the Ring Bearer yet, and they wanted me to tell you so they didn't have to keep anything from you. I felt terrible keeping it from you then and I feel even worse that it hurt you so much...that I hurt you so much.

I shouldn't have kept it from you. I shouldn't have pretended that I knew what kind of guy Jackson was. I should have told you it was me. If you'll give me a chance, I'll spend as much time as it takes proving to you that I'm the Ring Bearer that you know from the letters we've exchanged for the last 8 years. I'm Jax, the kid who wrote you when you were in the hospital. I'm Jackson, a kid who's growing up and learning how to show up in the world. You can call me whatever comes out, whatever you feel comfortable calling me.

I love you so much, Marley.

Please write me back.

The Ring Bearer

CHAPTER SIX
MARLEY & JAX,
AGE 18

Jax:

When the doors of the elevator opened up, there she was. Right in front of me. The girl I'd wanted to take to prom since we were little kids. My lungs heaved air out and I forgot to inhale. I couldn't look away. Only at her. The girl I should've taken to prom. Her presence physically took my breath away. The girl I waited too late to ask to prom. My heart beat increased sharply - twice as fast as normal. And she was with him. I couldn't see anything that was happening beyond our bubble. And damnit if she wasn't a vision. I tried, for my date's sake, to stay straight faced when I saw her. But nearly everything in me still goes soft when I see Marley. I lose all ability to control what my face is saying, and it's that very reason that I ended up at our senior prom by myself.

Yep. I took one look at Marley that night and promptly got left by my date. There wasn't even a full 5 seconds between it happening. My heart was beating so loudly that I almost didn't hear her - my date, that is. She literally looked at me, said, "Really Jackson?" and then huffed away while typing something on her phone. I later found out from my date that I "looked like I loved her," whatever that meant.

Marley, just smiled at me, popped one eyebrow in my direction and looped her arm through the arm of her date. I didn't even chase after mine. I just let her go. Maybe it was cold but I figured I could apologize to her when we were back at school. But "my girl" was still at the dance and her smile was warming my entire soul. Like goo...I turned to goo. I needed to stay right where I was.

That was a night to remember for sure. I spent most of it trying to catch Marley's eye and sneaking some of our inside jokes to her through text. Sure he may have been the one to take her to prom, but I was the one who knew her heart and I'd give anything to see her smile - even my own date. When hers made the mistake of slipping away to the bathroom, I slid in to shoot my shot.

I gently placed a hand on her shoulder and asked her to dance. Surprisingly, she took me up on it. The music was loud with enough bass to control your breathing. We stood shoulder to shoulder on the outskirts of the dance floor. "YOU LOOK GREAT!" I shouted over the music.

Marley:

He shouted just as the DJ switched from one song to the next, "YOU LOOK GREAT!" It felt like all heads turned in our direction. In reality it was only those who were close enough to hear him, but it definitely drew attention nonetheless.

I looked from my periphery as he stood beside me, staring longingly in my direction. I wouldn't face him. It wasn't seeing the look of adoration that was my concern. Instead it was my face, I feared that would be too honest. Too sincere. Too damning. He'd already lost his prom date. I couldn't lose mine too. I was questioning my decision to accept his request for a dance, but this was Jax we're talking about. So anyway, that music went from a banger to a slow jam and I felt like I'd been set up. Jax, Jackson, was still staring down at me. You know how you can feel someone's eyes on you? His were boring a hole clear through to my soul.

I finally looked up at him to tell him I'd changed my mind about the dance, but nothing exited my lips. The words were right there on the tip of my tongue but I couldn't will them out. Instead, I watched as his eyes and face softened. My young knees almost gave out on me. All the butterflies had accompanied me to prom. It was likely their insistent fluttering that kept me upright, honestly. His hand touched mine and I lost all hope of being able to translate any of the gobbledegook that was rummaging around in my brain.

He led me out to the dance floor and respectfully placed a hand on my waist while maintaining ahold of the hand he used to guide me out there. I inched in closer to him with each 4 count. Soon we were pelvis to pelvis and Jax nuzzled his face against mine. We were out there dancing cheek to cheek which felt too close - not because I didn't like it, but because I wished he was my date, who I knew was probably on his way back from the bathroom. I pulled back a bit and gazed into his eyes as he carted me all over the floor. I flashed one quick smile in his direction then rested my head on his shoulder and proceeded to melt into him as we danced. He stopped roaming the floor and instead began to rock in place with me in his arms. Then Jax, in all of his Jackson glory, leaned near my ear and cracked a joke about one of the things that was most important to me.

"So I wasn't sure I was gonna get to dance at prom, you know - since my date left me."

I giggled into his chest, still absorbing the moment as much as I could.

"Marley," he paused - letting my name linger in the air until I looked up at him again. He peered down at me with so much love in his eyes that I cried. I don't even know where it came from. It just came rushing to the surface and promptly found the nearest exit from my eyelid. "That looked like a cleansing tear," he said while using the back of his finger to wipe my cheek dry without missing a beat on the dance floor. "So, I've asked you at least once a month for the last year and a half. Sometimes in person. Sometimes in a letter." His sway slowed to a near stop. "Can I take you out on that date now, Sweetheart?"

I looked up at him, assessing the look in his eyes and simultaneously wondering what mine said. I was ready to say yes. Finally, ready to say yes! I cleared my throat and nodded when the words just wouldn't come out.

"Did you say something, Marley?" He asked me as something caught his eye and his demeanor quickly shifted from excitement to exasperation. He looked down into my eyes and spoke. "This was more than I could ask for tonight. Thanks for the dance."

Before I could say a thing, I was being tapped on the

shoulder by my date - who I'd honestly forgotten I had. That's the kind of hold Jackson had on me. He let his lingering finger contact speak for itself as I switched dance partners. I placed my cheek against my date's shoulder so I wouldn't have to face him, then watched as Jackson in his fancy tuxedo confidently strolled back to his table and sat down without any fanfare. Our eyes locked and I felt like I was still dancing with him. My date was holding me the same way that Jax had as we danced, but it just didn't feel the same. The care and tenderness was missing. I could feel the weight of Jackson's touch lingering on my back long after our dance was over. That moment is when I knew I needed to tell him.

I so wanted Jax to ask me to prom. I had dropped hints left and right, through letters and in person, but I assumed they just landed on deaf ears and blind eyes. By the time he finally asked me, a week before prom, I had already said yes to my date's ask. That left me in the position I was in that night, at the pinnacle event of one's high school experience with a date that I kind of thought was probably a decent enough kid. Nobody deserves that. I should've just told him no thank you. He deserved to go to prom with someone who wanted to go with him, not someone who just wanted to go with a date. To this day I still feel like I owe him an apology.

Well, there I was, dancing with Decent Date and staring into the eyes of the only person I really wanted to be dancing with. He mouthed a message to me from his table, "love you." I closed my eyes and smiled, allowing my date's dress shirt to catch the tears that fell. When I opened them again guess who was there, tapping my date on the shoulder to cut in.

Decent Date, who was seemingly more annoyed that

I'd cried on his shirt than anything else, stepped aside and Jax - Jackson, stepped in to resume his dance. The exhale that departed his chest as he wrapped his strong arms around me felt like one of contentment and it matched what I was feeling inside. His arms felt like home. I gazed into his eyes as we slow danced to a fast song. Unhurriedly, he leaned his face towards mine and whispered in my ear, "So about that date..." I chuckled during the pause, still lost in his energy - waiting for the rest of his message. "Was that a yes, Marley?"

"Yes, Jackson, but it better be a special date. I've waited almost 10 years for this."

He kissed the crown of my head, "Nothing but the best for you, Sweetheart." His cheek followed the path of his lips, resting squarely atop my head. "Nothing but the best."

Jax:

I didn't know what to do with myself. She became my unofficial prom date. We spent the rest of the night on the dance floor, dancing around each other's energy. I just wanted to be in her presence. I was a better person because of her and she finally trusted me enough to let me take her out on a date. I took a selfie of us while we were dancing and sent it to my Godfather with the message, "she said yes."

He called almost immediately. I declined the first two calls. Marley encouraged me to answer the FaceTime. I hit the accept button as we made our way back to the table, hand in hand.

"Jax. Lookin' sharp Godson! What did you do?"

"Hi Mr. Charlie! What do you mean?" I turned the camera so Marley could say hello.

"I mean, what did you do. Hi Marley-Mar! Don't you look beautiful."

"Hi Mr. Hughes! Thank you."

"Are you safe?"

"Yes, we're safe, sir," I replied.

"Okay, great, but I was talking to Marley. Are you safe?"

She laughed, "Yes, I'm safe!"

"Good. So what did you say yes to exactly? Are y'all at prom?"

We heard the voice of Dr. Chris in the background, "Charlie! Are you on a FaceTime call with them while they're at prom? Wait did they go together?"

"You heard her! We have questions," he said.

"We didn't come together. I lost my date the second I saw Marley step off the elevator, and Marley's date...well," I looked at Marley and shrugged my shoulders. Her head tossed from side to side. If only I could read her mind.

He looked at us incredulous, "How?"

"She texted me that I looked at Marley like I loved her."

A quick smirk decorated his face. "Well you do look at her like that, Jax," he said matter-of-fact.

"I mean, I do love her so I'm not surprised."

Marley, wiped a tear away from her face. I turned towards her and wiped her cheek dry then tilted my head in the direction of the phone and spoke to my Godfather, all while still gazing at my girl.

"Okay, so we gotta go."

"Jackson C. Williamson!"

"I have a date to plan, Mr. Charlie. She said yes."

"Now you know you can't just send me a text like that. I thought you were about to cash in on all those lessons we had on how to treat a wife, and elope or something. Y'all be safe and have fun - in that order."

"You too!" I joked while heavily considering the elopement part as I eyed my girl and ended the call. "So whaddya think?" I asked her, eyes still fixed on her face.

She raised her eyebrows at me and I noticed her ears shift position, as if she were attempting to listen better. "About what, Jax?"

"About the rest of the night," I chickened out. I knew that time didn't matter. It was becoming more and more clear to me as the night progressed that she was my person. "More dancing?"

"My ankles have hit their curfew, Jax."

"Do you need me to carry you to your - wait, did you ride with ole boy?"

"I did and I left my change of shoes in his..." before she could finish her sentence, he was at the table delivering her sneakers. "Thank you, Jason."

I stood up and bro hugged him. "Respect, man."

"Yeah, I just didn't want her to say I kept 'em," he said before turning and walking away.

She waited until he was out of sight. "So how did you and Lola get here, Jax?"

"I drove us, but I haven't seen her since the elevator." I looked around the room for her. "I mean she literally disappeared after texting me that."

"That you looked like you loved me?"

"Yeah, I mean she wasn't wrong in what she saw, Marley. You took my breath away."

She shook her head at me. "Jax."

"What? Just speaking what's on my mind." She looked like there was slight discomfort - probably caused by my lack of filter. "Can I help you change your shoes?" I asked, trying to change the subject to something lighter.

She lifted her right leg and positioned it on the seat,

between my legs. The slit on her dress fell open, exposing the curves of her calf and a portion of her thigh. The overly hormonal teenage boy in me was fighting to keep it respectful, but honestly I just wanted to slowly caress the entirety of her leg. I focused all my energy and I do mean ALL of my energy, on her foot. I unfastened the strap across her ankle then while lightly holding just below her calf muscle, gently pulled the shoe towards me and placed her foot back on the seat. I motioned for her to hand me the sneaker. She didn't move.

"Marley..." I said as I lifted my gaze from her foot to her eyes.

The intensity of her, "Jackson..." sent a shockwave through my body.

Nervous laughter escaped my mouth. "May I have your sneaker ma'am?"

She handed me the left shoe. I'm sure it was intentional because of the smirk on her face when I struggled to get it on her foot. She knew how to get me all worked up and I loved how she teased me.

I sat the left shoe on the floor beside my chair and motioned for the other one, all while smiling at my girl. She nearly handed me the shoe but instead winced like she was in pain and rubbed the outside of her ankle before I could grab it.

My instinct was to protect her, to soothe whatever was hurting. It's the reason I jumped up so quickly to cut in again on the dance with her date. It's also the reason I ended up massaging her ankle until it felt "all better," before putting on and lacing up her sneaker. Copy and paste the same process for her left leg - minus the baring of the thigh meat. If I wasn't already hooked on her heart, she would've gotten me that night. Thank goodness for the letters...

I carried her heels to the car as we left prom. I opened the car door for her and made sure she was in safely before I made my way back to the driver's side. She told me she wasn't ready to go home but didn't have any suggestions on where to go. So I drove her to my favorite spot in the city - the lake.

I parked the car in a cove near the water and grabbed my winter blanket from the trunk on my way to help her out of the car. The blanket was there to protect our clothes from any dirt that might've been waiting for us on the hood of the car, but it was a little chilly near the water. I draped my tuxedo jacket onto Marley's bare shoulders then helped her into a seated position on top of the car itself. For some mystical reason though, I found myself being drawn to the water's edge.

The moon was reflecting off the water and I spent a lot of time wondering how the water could be so still that it looked like glass. There we were in the stillness of the night. No music. Just nature's soundtrack. Before I knew it she was close to me, one arm wrapped around me from behind. I looked down at her face, shimmering in the moonlight and welcomed her body under my wing.

"Thank you for tonight, Marley," I told her. She raised up on her tiptoes and planted a tender kiss on my cheek. Her face. I can still see her sweet face as she looked up at me with so much love. That's when it hit me. It's highly likely that's what my date saw before she ditched me and that's probably what Marley was looking at in that very moment.

I was so grateful that my friend, my best friend, was standing with me at the lake instead of my date. I was feeling full of love. And when she pressed her body into mine, I was feeling full of something else too.

My resolve was tested a lot that night, but I can proudly say I passed. Not even so much as a first kiss. Just a lot of snuggles near the water, a lot of face nuzzles under the blanket, a lot of hand holding as we stared up at the stars from the hood of the car, and a lot of peace within.

Good Morning, Marley,

Prom was perfect.

I had trouble sleeping when I got home. I could still feel your arms hugging me. I could still smell your scent on my skin. I found myself replaying that dance on a loop in my head and staring out my window at the stars. I didn't know it would be like this. I didn't know I would be like this. I used to laugh at the way my Godfather would melt around his wife. I didn't see that coming for me, but I'm here now.

What have you done to me, Shy Girl? Do we need to go back and rewrite the origin story of Awkward Man? I think this might be more accurate than what's in that comic.

I can't wait to see you on Friday night. I'll pick you up at 6:00 from the address listed on your envelopes. Dinner, mini golf and go carts, just like you asked for when we were 12. If that's okay, let me know at school.

I love you, Sweetheart!

Please write me back.

Jackson

p.s. I hope your Dad likes me.

Hi Jackson,

I agree. Prom was perfect. I had some amazing dreams that night too, but none of them compared to what I got to actually experience with you that night. Our first dance together was even better than I expected. You got all the moves!

I didn't do anything to you, but I've been thinking about you nonstop since you dropped me off that night. Maybe the better question is what did you do to me?

I can hardly wait for our date. My Dad said you better make it 5:30 so he can have a Man to Man talk with you. Also, can we add ice cream in there somewhere? Dad didn't ask that. I'm asking for myself. I left that out of my letter when I was 12. LOL.

Love you lots.

Your favorite girl,
Marley

CHAPTER SEVEN
MARLEY & JAX,
AGE 18

Marley:

My insides fluttered as I waited by my bedroom window to see his car pull into our driveway. These weren't normal butterflies though. Imagine a school of bass fish spawning in the lake on a warm summer day. These were big flutters we're talking about here. The kind that make you take notice of what's going on. And that's exactly what my body did. All my senses were heightened as I waited for Jax to arrive. He pulled into the driveway at 5:25, ready to chat with my dad. I bolted from my room, then waited at the top of the steps for the doorbell to ring. Dad, on his way to the door, snickered as he noticed my anxious state.

"Baby girl, breathe with me," he said before taking three consecutive deep breaths and exhales. I breathed with him and went back into my room where I waited on the bed with the door ajar so I could hear what was happening downstairs. Dad unlocked the front door.

I heard Jax greet Dad, "Hello sir."

Then Dad to Jax, "Young man. You must be Jax."

"Yes sir, Jackson Williamson, sir."

"Come in, let's have a seat in the living room here."

Their footsteps got louder as they walked along the hardwoods my parents had restored right after they found out about Mom's diagnosis.

"So, Jackson, you've been writing to Marley for a while now."

"Yes sir. I was 7 years old when I wrote her the peace dove."

"And you're what, about 18 now?"

"Yes sir."

"Legal age." There was silence. I could only assume that Jax must have nodded. "So is my daughter." Again, silence. "How do you feel about Marley, Jackson?"

"Sir?"

"How do you FEEL about my daughter, son?"

"I love her, sir."

"Mmm hmm. I gathered that from all the letters. When you're young, love feels simple. But sometimes that changes. What does love mean to you now?"

"Well," Jackson started before clearing his throat. "Love is...a choice we make to show someone how much we care about them. If we love someone, we support them when times are hard. We celebrate with them when things are good. We listen to why they're mad if they're willing to tell us about it. We go the extra mile to add more happiness to their life and try not to add more stress than necessary. We let them be, when they need it, and we respect what they're feeling, even if we don't feel the same way about something."

"Uh huh," Dad paused. "When she's talked to me about a Jackson in the last year or so, initially he wasn't someone I would describe as very loving. Was that you or a different Jackson?"

"No sir, it was me."

"I see. So what's different now than the Jackson who showed the opposite of love to Marley?"

"Marley challenged me to be myself instead of some version that I thought the other kids would like and respect."

"And how did that work out for you?"

"It's so much easier to show up as is than trying to remember all the fake stuff I'm supposed to do."

"So Marley obviously trusts you now because she agreed to go on a date with you. How am I supposed to trust you though?"

"I'll earn your trust sir. If you'll let me show you who I really am, if you'll let me date Marley, like old-fashioned dating, I promise to treat her with love and respect."

The quiet that hung out in the main floor was deafening. How could silence be THAT loud? I heard a foot tapping on the floor. I'd have bet money that was Dad's thinking foot. He did that often.

Dad called up to me, "Marley, Jackson is here to take you out on a date."

I took three more deep breaths and slowly opened my bedroom door. Jackson, still seated on the couch in the living room looked up towards the staircase and let out a shallow breath as soon as we made eye contact.

"Uh oh," Dad said and started laughing as he stood up to greet me. "You've got it bad, son."

Jackson chuckled as he stood up and walked towards the bottom of the stairs to greet me. When he wrapped his arms around me and rested his cheek atop my head I was home. I mean I felt comfortable in the house that I shared with Dad. It was familiar. But it wasn't until I was cocooned in Jackson's arms that the house felt like home. I'm fairly certain that I let out a languished murmur. My knees were weak and I just wanted to live inside that feeling.

He handed me a plastic container that held a single wrist corsage. "If I would've asked you to prom sooner, I would've bought one of these for you to wear," he said as he opened up the clamshell container and slipped the corsage on my wrist. It wriggled around on my arm a bit. "Does it fit?"

The sweet scent of the purple hydrangeas and red carnations wafted towards my nostrils. "It fits perfectly, Jax. Thank you." I felt like I was blushing underneath my melanated skin. He had gotten me a wrist corsage that looked just like the one I wore to the Hughes' wedding, and it included my favorite color. I couldn't believe he remembered that.

"Are you ready?" he asked me, that intense stare reeling me in even further.

I looked at Dad, who nodded in my direction. "Yes, Jax. Thank you, Dad!"

He walked us to the front door, watched as Jackson opened the car door for me, waited as the two of us buckled our seatbelts and stood witness as we drove off on our adventure together.

Jax:

I didn't know whether or not I was coming or going. I tried to steel my nerves, but I was talking to my future father in law - only he didn't know it yet. He asked me if I was the jerk that was being an ass towards his daughter and I knew I had to fess up to it. I was so nervous my foot was tapping on the floor and no matter how hard I tried, it wouldn't stop. It was so loud on those hardwoods too. He was just lookin me over, like he was trying to decide if he should entrust his child with this hormonal young adult. He was right to consider it. It was hard to restrain myself around Marley.

When she came down the steps I had to remind myself that I was in the presence of her father. It didn't matter what she wore, it was her energy that constantly took my breath away and drew me in like a magnet. All I wanted to do was hold her in my arms. I didn't want to move. She just felt like home. That's the easiest way for me to describe it. It's not that we were just comfortable with each other. I think we were comfortable with each other because we were supposed to be. But that first date....man, that first date would not have you believing that at all. It started off perfect. I gave her the corsage. Opened the car door for her. We drove off together, headed towards easily one of the roughest nights of my life to that point.

The second we turned off of her street it began. We almost got run over by a cop car on a silent run. All I could think was that I had just asked this man to entrust his child with me and I almost got her killed on my watch. Then I was overly cautious - so much so that we were late for dinner. Marley was hungry. I was hungry. We were both a bit irritable.

Marley:

I was hangry. I couldn't figure out why Jax was driving so slowly. He missed his reservation, so they gave us a choice to either reschedule for the next day or wait 45 minutes until a table opened up after their last reservation. I tried not to cuss him out with my eyes. I know he wasn't purposefully trying to miss it. But I was so hungry! I think he got the point, so we ended up leaving the restaurant and going to the closest fast food joint nearby. Sonic. I couldn't tell if he was disappointed or upset or mad at me. I was just grateful to have food in my belly. Plus their slushes didn't miss. So there I was, sitting on the passenger side of my best friend's ride, my belly full, slurpin' on a fruit punch slush, my heart happy - almost all was right with the world.

Jax:

I was upset and embarrassed. I was trying so hard to be careful with her in the car that I missed our reservation. We either had to wait 45 minutes or go somewhere else. She looked annoyed and impatient, so I just said let's try again later. I only wanted the best for her. I didn't want to go to Sonic. I mean, don't get me wrong, Sonic is okay, but I promised Marley and her Dad the best. So we went from eating at a reserved table to our own private car stall. I was bombing this date and there was so much pressure to save it that my head was hurting. I barely ate anything and I hardly looked in her direction. I couldn't bare to face a look of disappointment. I remember letting out a deep sigh and feeling Marley's hand on my shoulder. My head followed her arm and eventually my eyes traced up to meet hers. I could see the whole world in there. She nodded in my direction and I finally broke my silence.

Marley:

He looked so stressed out, so I rubbed his shoulder, just trying to relieve some of the stress. When I touched him, his head snapped in my direction and his eyes trailed slowly up my arm, eventually finding their way to mine. Those ojazos marrón. It felt like the source of the universe was found in those big brown eyes of his. Yep, I could see galaxies in there and I nodded in confirmation that what I was seeing was real. I almost snapped out of my trance as soon as he spoke.

His tone, ultra melancholy. "Hey, sorry about dinner. I thought we could go to the mini golf course at the art museum afterward, but if you just want to go home, I understand."

I was still gazing into the 3rd billionth light year in Jax's eyes when I mumbled my answer, "Mini golf is fine."

Jax:

So there I was sitting in the car, looking into the eyes of the girl I loved, listening to her apathy about going to play mini golf. It felt like she was taking pity on me. I don't know what I expected, but it wasn't that. I started to back the car out of the stall and nearly hit a carhop. They tapped on the side of the door as they somehow skated out of the way of my absent-minded driving.

I checked for any other people or cars and backed out of the space, then headed out onto the streets again, slowly, on our way to the art museum. We miraculously found a spot on the street just beside the museum lawn. I opened Marley's car door and helped her out of my ride.

We walked hand in hand towards the stand to purchase our tickets, but nobody was there. In fact, nobody was on the course at all. It was closed. It was at that point that I felt totally defeated by this date. Nothing that I planned had worked out. I felt like I couldn't be the man I wanted to be for Marley.

Marley:

Mini golf was closed but I thought it would be cool to sit and watch traffic drive by. It didn't matter what we were doing. I just wanted to spend time with Jackson. He was putting so much pressure on himself though. I could feel it in the way he brushed off holding my hand. I could sense it in the way he walked back to the car in silence. It was highly visible as he closed my car door and walked to the driver's side, tapping his fist on his forehead. When he got in the car, put his seatbelt on and drove away from the museum without a word, I was worried.

Jax:

I could feel the stress building to a breaking point, but I didn't want to show her that I was weak. My shoulders felt tighter and tighter, probably because I had raised them up near my ears trying to hold in the tears that were burning my eyes. Eventually it all became too much. I blinked one time and my face was flooded with the results of holding in stress instead of letting it out. I signaled, turned right into a desolate parking lot and pulled successfully into a spot without a near miss of hitting or getting hit by anyone or anything. I buried my face in my hands and sobbed. I couldn't control it. My body was trying to cleanse my soul of all the toxic mess I'd been holding in.

In the midst of my breakdown I heard the volume of the stereo increase, and the passenger door unlock, open and close. I was convinced I had blown my shot. I had asked her to trust me and then I took her on what felt like the most terrible date in the world. "Nothing but the best for you," I had promised her. But I gave her the worst and she had turned up the volume, I thought, to drown out my cries.

My face was still buried in my hands when I heard my door open. She tapped me on the shoulder, but I couldn't look up at her. I was embarrassed to have cried in front of her, to have failed so deeply in front of her.

"Ring bearer..." she called to me as she tapped my shoulder once more.

"Yes, Marley," I mumbled into my hands.

"Can I have this dance?" she asked me. I thought she had to be kidding. My eyes still full of tears, I looked up at her. She extended her flower adorned hand towards me. "Love adds light and life. Remember?"

"I messed up our first date, Marley."

She was calm. "I'm right here, Ring Bearer. The date is still happening." Her face lit up as she smiled in my direction, "The only way you'll mess it up is if you turn me down for this dance."

I had to be the luckiest dude walking the earth that night. That's how I felt anyway. I stepped out of the car and closed the door. The music was loud enough that we could still hear it as the K-Ci and JoJo started singing their classic hit, "All My Life."

I didn't think I could love her anymore, but Marley gave me space to let my guard down and still feel safe while doing it. I lowered my forehead onto hers, my eyes closed, still feeling vulnerable and grateful simultaneously. We danced together in that empty parking lot, just the two of us and some slow jams from our parents' generation.

Her arms wrapped around my neck and one hand caressing the base of my head, she softly spoke, "Jax, you're one of my favorite people in the whole wide world."

My body felt like it folded into her arms. The person I thought I was supposed to be went flying out the window when I cried in front of her in the car. The person I was becoming while I was around her was far better. She gave me space to be frustrated and sad, and didn't emasculate me for having and expressing my feelings.

"What do you need?" she whispered.

I finally conjured up some words that barely made it out of my mouth, "Just this...just you."

Her voice a bit more audible than before, "Do you feel it?"

"Feel what Sweetheart?" I asked softly.

There was silence. She hadn't said anything but had slowly stopped dancing. I opened my eyes as she wiped anew the space on my cheeks where my tears had rolled. I thought the silence in her Dad's house was loud, but this was a different type of silence entirely. Everything else had faded away. It was just the two of us, in our own bubble floating through time and space. I'm not sure how long we gazed into each other's eyes. I'm not sure how long time was suspended. I only remember repeating my question to her, "Feel what Sweetheart?" and watching light fill her eyes.

I never did get an answer from her, or maybe I didn't hear it because my hormonal urges had resurfaced. I tried to fight it. I tried to internally rationalize it away. But my mouth moved faster than my brain.

"Marley..." our eyes were locked on each other.

Those pupils of hers were dilated again. "Mm hmm..."

I knew the rest of the date was bad so asking this was going to be a risk. I slowly inhaled through my nose and held my breath. "Can I kiss you?"

She took her sweet time answering me, "yes, Jackson." Leaned up against the door of my car, I pulled her in closer to me and hugged her tight, our bodies fitting together like puzzle pieces. My hands roamed up her back, traced along her neck, and lifted from her frame just long enough for me to gently cup her face. I took my sweet time savoring the taste of her lips and pouring my love into her.

Once I had let go of the pressure of the first date, things were easy again. We were vibing as strong as we had been at prom. I still kept it respectful, knowing that I still had to safely return somebody's daughter to them at the end of the night.

She was my girl and nobody could tell me any differently.

We spent the next few weeks as close to each other as possible. I knew, we both did, that our time together in the same city was drawing short. Our individual plans after graduation were going to test our new relationship. If we weren't hanging out in her Dad's living room, we were on the phone for hours. If we weren't in each other's space at school, we were writing letters to each other to fill the void.

Marley:

As the week of graduation approached, I found myself sitting in feelings I didn't know what to do with. I was grateful for high school to be finished so I could move on to what's next. I was melancholy because I knew that my best friend and I had one summer left together before everything was going to change. I was excited about starting school away from Kansas City in the fall. I was nervous about leaving Dad by himself. I wished Mom was here to see this milestone. I was heartbroken at the thought of my guy being a thousand miles away. I was all over the place emotionally.

When graduation day arrived, Jackson picked me up to drive us to the soccer stadium for our ceremony. Dad handed him a card and hugged him tightly. "I'm so proud of you, son," he told him, holding on for a bit longer than normal. "I'll find you for pictures after the ceremony, but you take care of our girl tonight, okay?"

Jackson had tears in his eyes as he answered, "Yes sir!"

They had become pretty close in the last few weeks. Dad even had a different type of light in his eyes. It was one I hadn't seen since Mom had passed. I was so thankful that they'd have each other when I left for school. But that moment, watching the two of them add light to each other's life, is one that I'll hold onto forever. One would think it's because it was so moving. I mean that was part of it. In reality though, it's because of what happened next.

I squeezed Dad tightly and said goodbye, then told him that I'd see him once I had graduated and started towards the front door. Before I could get there though, Jackson grabbed ahold of my hand as I passed by, lacing his fingers between mine in the process, and asked me to, "Hold on Mar." When I turned around he was in the process of getting down on one knee and I just knew that I was about to wake up from a dream.

"Jackson, stop playing, we have to go!" I said as I tugged on his hand.

"Marley, I'm not playing," he said, as a smile spread across his entire face. "You know I'm serious when it comes to you, when it comes to us."

I looked up at Dad, who nodded towards Jax, as if he were asking me to listen to him.

I looked down towards my best friend, who was waiting patiently for me to return his gaze.

"Marley, I know we've only officially been together for a month, but you've been my girl since I saw you at my Godparents' wedding. You know me better than anybody else and I hope you feel I know you the same way. You're my best friend and my forever love. I haven't been too good about asking you about important things in a timely manner, so before things get hectic after we graduate, I want you to know that I'll always be yours if you'll have me." Jackson reached into the pocket of his vest and pulled out the card that Dad had just handed him. He ran his finger underneath the fold of the envelope and tilted the entire thing until something shiny fell into his left hand. He cupped it in his palm, held it to his heart and cleared his throat before presenting the ring to me between his thumb and pointer finger. "Will you have me, Mar?"

I was looking down at my Mom's ring. Dad was in on the whole thing. That explained the light in his eyes. That explained the emotional hug. That explained why Dad wasn't taking me to graduation himself and why he asked me if Jackson was going to drive us. I could feel my heart pulsing in my eyes. I forgot to breathe. I stooped down in front of Jackson held his face in my hands and gazed into his eyes.

His left hand suddenly dropped down to his knee. "Marley...breathe Sweetheart," he whispered with concern in his voice. I took a deep breath and kissed him like we were already standing at the altar.

"Soooooo, was that a yes then?" Jax asked as Dad chuckled in the background.

"It's a yes, Ring Bearer!" I said before he eagerly slipped the ring onto my left third finger and stood up, lifting me off the ground and spinning us around in one seamless move.

The doorbell rang and Dad opened the door to greet Mr. Charlie and Dr. Chris. Jax looked at them and nodded before dropping his forehead onto mine and presenting my newly adorned hand to them. We were surrounded with love from everyone who was physically present in the house and those who were not. We quickly took photos and drove towards our graduation ceremony so we could line up with all of our classmates.

The windows were down and the music was up as we drove towards our future. Jackson glanced over at me at every stoplight, his lower lip tucked underneath his top teeth. Knowing that we had each other's backs for the rest of our lives brought an unexpected level of contentment. I thoroughly loved and was in love with that guy, and all my love came pouring out in the form of kisses every time he tucked that lip.

"Sweetheart, you're making me want to pull the car over. You gotta let me drive without all this temptation and distraction."

Truth be told, I wanted him to pull the car over. If our family wasn't expecting to see us walk across the stage, I would've kissed him again and dared him to do it. Instead

I giggled and told him I wouldn't kiss him again until the car was parked. Once we arrived though, you would've thought we hadn't seen each other in months. Jax rolled up the windows and left the car running. Prince started singing about Diamonds and Pearls and the way Jax held my heart with just one glance. I was already done for, then he said it, "I get to love you forever," and I met him in the middle of the car to show him just how much I loved him.

One of Jax's friends knocked on the driver's window, "Come on lovebirds, you're gonna be late for graduation!"

We stared at each other as the kissing stopped and that's when the laughter started. I'm not even sure that we were laughing at anything in particular. I think we were just two giddy kids. We hopped out of the car, our cap and gown in hand. He helped me put on my cap as I zipped up his gown. Then we switched. I helped him put on his cap and straightened his tassel as he zipped up my gown. Once everything was orderly, we took one quick selfie together and held hands as we trotted towards the stadium like the rest of the stragglers.

As we got closer to the stadium, Jax slowed down and took in the moment. We stopped just inside the entryway, right as school staff was asking people to get in line as we had practiced the day before. Jax turned to me and placed my hand lovingly over his heart. "Breathe with me?" he asked. I nodded anxiously as we were about to take the first of several big steps towards our life together.

Jackson led us through three deep breaths, kissed the back of my hand then whispered into my ear "I'll see you in there Sweetheart."

"Love you lots, Ring Bearer," I told him. Our grasp lingered from palm to fingertips as we parted ways to join our respective lines.

We texted each other during the graduation ceremony.

"Where are you, Sweetheart?"

"Left side. 10th row back. 2nd from the outside. u?"

"Right side. 10th row back. 2nd from the inside."

"I see you."

"You're so beautiful."

"Thank you my handsome, Ring Bearer."

"I think it's time for an upgrade from Ring Bearer, Marley."

"Groom to Be doesn't have the same ring to it, Jackson."

"Mar..."

"Jax..."

"I can't wait to kiss you again. How much longer until it's over?"

"I can't wait to..."

"Stop."

"ijs"

"Whatchu just sayin?"

"You know what I'm saying, Ring Bearer..."

"Tell me, Mar," he waited until I read the text then leaned forward and looked towards the opposite side of the field at me. I suppressed my smile as we looked at each other. He bit his lip again.

"Bring those over here to me, mister."

"Mrs. Williamson! Pay attention to the speaker ma'am."

I stopped texting him and pretended to listen to the speaker. I knew it was just a matter of time before he sent another text.

"Okay, I change my mind. Text me?"

"Shh...the Valedictorian is speaking."

"Oh, so we're shushing each other now, huh?"

"Sorry, Jackson. Someone asked me to pay attention to the speaker. Come get me when this is done."

The speaker finished. They called our names and we each had our high school moment of glory as we walked across the stage to collect our diplomas. Then they had us officially move our tassels, pronounced that we were officially finished with our K-12 experience, presented our class to the world, and people chucked their caps in the air. I never understood that. I pretended to toss mine and then held it in my hand. While our classmates went to collect their caps, Jackson came to collect me. He came straight down Row 10, wrapped me up from behind and kissed me on the crown of my head.

Dad had grabbed a seat with the Hughes Family and they all met us on the concourse after the ceremony had concluded. We still had plans to attend grad night. But we knew they were ready to take lots of photos.

"Were you two texting during the whole graduation?" Dr. Chris asked me.

I laughed, "maybe half of it?"

She shook her head before telling me, "You weren't the only two on your phones."

"We weren't?" I asked, then laughed as she showed me a picture on her phone.

"Mr. Charlie, your soon-to-be Godfather, shared this picture with me."

Not one head was looking in the direction of the speaker. All were down looking at their phones or up looking towards the families in the audience. Then there was Jax and I - looking across the rows smiling at each other.

"You two have always had a strong connection, Marley. I saw you watching him during our wedding reception and he was busy trying to work up the nerve to go talk to you. Remember when you were babysitting for us? I could see it before we left - probably before you even realized it was there, and it was definitely strong when we got back. Then there was prom. Mr. Charlie called because it wasn't inconceivable that the two of you would elope." She laughed and continued. "I bet people probably comment on it a lot, don't they?"

I nodded, unsure of what else to say. We definitely got looks from classmates, retail staff, school staff, pretty much anyone we encountered. It wasn't a bad look at all, but there was usually an "awww," that accompanied it.

"I know you just got engaged and you're probably not even thinking about a date right now. Just know you don't have to rush the wedding, kiddo. The two of you will know when the time is right. Don't let other people tell you when it's supposed to happen for you."

I hugged her and held on as tightly as I could. I'm not sure if she knew it or not, but Dr. Chris had been like a mother figure to me for the last 4 years. "Thank you for everything," I told her.

"You're very welcome, Marley. I'm so proud of you!" she said as she squeezed me back. "Can't wait to see how you impact the world, kiddo."

Dad and Jax wrapped up their conversation and joined us on the sidewalk. Dr. Chris and I shook pinkies as we were accustomed to doing. Then the photos commenced. Me and Dad. Me and The Hughes. Me and Jax. Jax and The Hughes. Jax and Dad. Me, Jax, and Dad. Me, Jax, and The Hughes. Dad and The Hughes. All of us together. So many photos. There towards the end, all I could think about was those who weren't with us; my mom and Jax's parents.

I think Jax must've noticed the shift. He swooped in behind me, wrapped me up in his arms and rested his chin on my shoulder. I tilted my head towards his and closed my eyes as our temples touched. Jackson proceeded to breathe deeply with me. Inhale. Exhale. Repeat. Three sets.

"You about ready to head to grad night?" he whispered in my ear. I nodded. He continued, his voice deep and soft, "Are we really going to grad night, Marley?"

I giggled and nodded again. He nodded and chuckled, then whispered softly in my ear, "hmmm...you sure?" I couldn't keep a straight face. Jackson laughed and whispered, "Let's go, sweetheart." The warmth of his breath tickled my inner ear and goosebumps jumped to the surface of my neck.

Mr. Charlie had been watching Jax the entire time. "Look at these two canoodling over here. You better be good to her, Jax."

"Nothing but the best!" Jax told him.

Jax:
I finally got to ask her the question that'd been slowly burning a hole in me since I read her second letter to me. I didn't know what it would look like to build a life with someone, but I was willing to give it a shot. I loved her with every bone in my body.

About a week before graduation, when I asked her Dad for his permission, he only asked me two questions.

One, "When things get hard, and you feel like you don't like her very much in that moment, what's your plan?" I told him that I'd seen my parents fight with each other as I grew up and that I wanted to find something similar to what they did. Dad would tell Mom that he needed a minute to cool off and she would still be frustrated but would agree and give him space. He would take an hour to calm down and then check in with her to see when she was available to finish talking about things.That's what I wanted in a marriage. Someone who would be willing to push me to become my best and someone who was willing to receive the same in return. That was Marley.

His second question caught me off guard and brought tears to my eyes. "Would you like to present her with her mother's ring?" I told him that I couldn't possibly do that and he insisted. I offered to pay him for it and he refused. He told me that he'd get it to me on graduation day. The night before I had trouble sleeping. I knew that I was gonna propose the next day. He knew it. My godparents knew it. We just had the timing all wrong.

The plan was for me to propose right after the graduation ceremony. I was going to do it in front of our entire class. But the night before, my eyes wide open as I lay restless in the bed, I thought about Marley and what it might be like for her if that's how I chose to propose. It just didn't seem like something she'd like. I thought it would be a better fit for her if it were quiet and around the person she loved most, her Dad. I sent him and my Godfather a text late at night so they would know what the modified plan was. They both sent back a thumbs up. And with that, I found myself more able to rest. It didn't happen as I'd hoped, but I was definitely less stressed.

That morning, I tried to treat it as a normal day even though it was anything but. This was the day that I finished high school. This was the day that I became a functioning member of society. This was the day I was going to propose to the love of my life. I called her that morning to wish her a happy graduation day and we were on the phone for a solid 2 hours. Just chatting about nothing and everything all at once. We were content just listening to each other breathe and being in the same space - even if that space wasn't physically in the same room. That solidified my desire to propose. That we didn't need to be in continual conversation, that we could just be around each other without needing to force a conversation, that we were still just as content in the silence, was all I needed for reassurance that the question I was about to ask her in a few hours, was the right question in the right time.

Driving to her house felt like it took twice as long as normal, and no I hadn't slowed down like I did on our first date. It felt like the longer I drove, the more the road stretched out like taffy. It just kept extending. So I kept on driving, determined to get to my wife. Well, who I knew to be my wife anyway. Once I finally got there, I saw her peeking out of her bedroom window. She was waiting for me and I loved the look of contentment that fell over her when she saw me.

I waved to her and by the time I got to the front door, she was there to greet me with a hug. It was one of the warmest embraces I'd felt from her and I was putty in her arms. Her Dad handed me a hard and hugged me, letting me know that he was proud of me. I felt the ring inside the card and tucked it into the vest I was wearing. He whispered a message to me that Marley couldn't possibly have heard, "Ask her when you feel it in your heart, when you love her as she is, when you know for certain that you can add light to the world together."

I teared up, overwhelmed with so many emotions and thoughts, and having his blessing meant so much to me.

"Take care of our girl tonight," he told me and I just felt it, all of it - loving her as is, knowing that we add light together, it lingered in my heart both beforehand and in that moment. So as she started pressing onward in a rush towards the front door, I knew it was time to slow down, be more turtle like, soak up the moment and ask her. I grabbed her hand as she passed by and asked her to hold on. When I dropped to one knee, it looked like she knew what should have been coming, but I don't think she was expecting it. I asked if she'd have me and told her that I'd be hers forever. The world felt like it stopped spinning as I waited for her to answer me. I heard every breath as they worked their way through my body in slow motion.

Those hardwood floors felt more like concrete under my knee. She stared at the ring, dropped down to her knees and scooped up my face without saying a word. I continued to wait, and breathe, while her face said the opposite was happening for her. I had to ask her to breathe so she wouldn't pass out. It felt like she stole my oxygen as she kissed me. I felt a little bad kissing her like that in front of her Dad so in true awkward fashion, I cracked a joke. When she said yes and called me Ring Bearer, I thought I'd melt through the floorboards. I told you I turn to goo, right?

The light around her was brighter than I'd ever seen it. I spun her around in excitement. When we stopped, I saw my Godparents. I don't know how they got in Marley's house. I didn't even hear the doorbell ring or a knock at the door. Nothing. Now that I think about it, everything she said after yes was a blur. I think we took pictures there and then drove to the stadium for graduation. I didn't pay much attention during graduation, I just remember waiting for it to be over so I could get to my girl. When everybody tossed their caps in the air, I ran down the row to get to her, my favorite person in the world.

I know everybody believes that about their person, but everybody I know of who met Marley felt the same way about her. That's why I felt so lucky that she chose me. We took lots of pictures after graduation but I just wanted to celebrate our engagement. I checked a couple of times to see if she still wanted to go to Grad Night. I didn't care that I paid money to go. I felt like we could have better spent our time away from our classmates.

We went anyway. It was cool I guess. Looking back on it now, grad night feels like the beginning of the beginning of the end. That was a very short summer - much shorter than it was supposed to be.

ENGAGEMENT LETTERS
- MARLEY & JAX -
AGE 18

Good Morning Marley,

I love it when you cross my mind. I know we just saw each other, but I had a feeling I'd have a hard time telling you this in person. So, if you're reading this letter, just know that I tried, but I couldn't bring myself to sprinkle disappointment onto an otherwise perfect day.

You already know that I got accepted into the cyber security training program I told you about, and it was supposed to start the summer right after graduation. They just sent the details to my house. I thought it would start at the end of summer. It turns out though that the training begins in two weeks. You probably remember that the program requires me to be off the grid for six months. So I'm not going to be here to send you off to college like we originally thought, and like I had pictured in my mind.

I know the next six months might be tough for us, but it's an amazing opportunity for my career and our future. It will put me on the fast track to a job that will let me take care of you while you're in school and afterwards.

I believe in us and our love, and I'm sure we can get through anything together.

Let's cherish every moment this summer.

I love you, Sweetheart!
Jackson

Hi Jackson,

I'm so excited for you and your incredible opportunity in that training program! I know how much you want this and I couldn't be prouder of you.

Yes, the thought of being apart for six months is kind of disappointing and you leaving so soon is not what we expected but I believe in us, too. We'll make it work, I promise. Let's savor every second of this summer. Our love is strong enough to endure a temporary separation. If it helps ease some of what you fear you'll miss, you can help me pack some of my stuff away for college before you leave.

This summer is still going to be sweet as long as we're present when we're near each other.

I love you, Ring Bearer (Groom to Be? GTB?)

Forever yours,
Marley

Good Morning Marley,

I can hardly believe I've already been gone for a month. I miss you every day, and I spend a lot of time thinking about that last night at the lake. The water was so healing and so is your touch.

I can't believe how quickly the time is passing. I'm so grateful for the letters we exchange; they keep me connected to you even while I'm off the grid. Training is intense, and I'm learning so much, but I can't wait until I see you in December so I can tell you all about it.

I'm excited that they let you go early to take a few classes during the summer. I hope they're treating you well and that you're enjoying things. I know you. Get out there and meet people. Don't stay hidden in your room! I wish I could be there with you, but I know you'll do great things. Remember, you're the love of my life and my biggest inspiration.

Please write me back.

I love you endlessly,
Jackson

My Jackson,

I received your letter, and it brought a smile to my face amidst the hectic college life. Is it silly that I still wait to open them in the morning? It still builds excitement. I'm so proud of you and all the hard work you're putting into the cyber security program and I'm excited that the time is flying by. Your dedication inspires me every day and I know our future family will benefit from how much effort you put into everything.

College is both exciting and hard. I miss home. Summer classes flew by and now everybody is here on campus for the Fall semester. I'm making friends and getting involved in different activities, but nothing compares to the feeling of being with you. I can't wait for you to come pick me up in December, so we can be together again.

I love you so much more today than I did yesterday, my handsome man. Our love is exponential!

Always thinking of you,
Marley

Hi Jackson,

I have some really exciting news to share! I thought I could save it for when I saw you in December but that doesn't seem fair. I'd much rather tell you in person or on the phone Awkward Man, but I know you can't really do that right now.

I've been sick for the last few weeks and I finally went to the Health Center on campus. Turns out the lake was healing and very fruitful for us.

I'm pregnant with our child.

I'm overwhelmed with happiness and a lot of nervousness. I wish you were here to share this moment with me. I'm counting the days until I see you again and can hold you close.

If my countdown is right, you'll be finished with the training program in four months, and then we'll be able to spend the rest of our lives together. You're going to be an amazing Daddy, and I'm so grateful for the life we're building together.

All my love,

Marley

Good Morning Marley!

I've spoken to the program coordinators, and they're giving me a short leave to come and see you. Let's get married while I'm out! I'll be there in a few days, and we can figure everything out together. We're a team, Marley. We'll face whatever comes our way with love and determination.

I love our life so much!
Jackson

CHAPTER EIGHT
PRE-WEDDING RUSH
AGE 18

Jax:

They only gave me three days, then I had to be back at the training program. So I called Marley's Dad, my parents - who had finally gotten back from Dad's two-year stint overseas, and my Godparents. They told me they'd take care of the details and my job was to get a tux and get to Marley safely.

My flight to Maryland left early in the morning, but 4 hours later I was in the same state as my future wife. I cried so much on the flight that the flight attendant, a brotha who I guessed was in his 30s or 40s - it's hard to tell with us - asked me several times if I was okay. I finally unloaded everything and told him I was anxious because I wanted to see her, sad because she had to go through all of the doctor's appointments without me until I could finish that program, and happy because we were about to start our lives together. He encouraged me to write down what was on my mind so I could get it out and be clear headed and present for the actual wedding.

I wrote one letter on the plane so Marley could read it in the morning, before we got married.

I thought that was the best advice the flight attendant could've given me. But it turns out he gave me so much more. The news made its way to the flight captain who made an announcement mid-flight. Not only did the other passengers cheer, they also wrote out advice and best wishes on cocktail napkins from the snack cart that were bound in an envelope and delivered to me before I debarked the plane. I couldn't wait to share those with Marley as we got older. I figured I would leave a couple in the letters we sent to each other when I had to go back to the training program. I never got to send those to her though. They just stayed in the envelope.

Marley:
I got a phone call from Dad, checking to see if I received Jax's last letter. He gave me everybody's flight information for the coming weekend and asked if I would be able to find a dress before they got there.

I told him that I wasn't sure where to look and he told me that he'd take care of it. He got in a day before Jackson so we could spend a day together just Dad and Daughter. He picked me up from my residence hall and took me to breakfast at Miss Shirley's Cafe at Inner Harbor, then just a short drive away we made it to our appointment at Selah's for a wedding gown alteration. Dad had surprised me with Mom's wedding dress which made me a weepy mess. When I was younger, she and I would talk about how we'd get it altered so I could wear it on my wedding day. She used to tease me that it would be Jax that would be waiting for me at the end of the altar. I always thought she was joking, but maybe she instinctively knew.

That gown was a precious heirloom, brimming with memories of love and happiness. I was honored to get the chance to wear it. As I slipped into the dress for them to take measurements, I couldn't help but feel a profound connection to my mother. The ivory silk adorned with delicate lace draped nearly perfectly from my frame. They clipped wooden pins in the areas where it would be taken in and I felt comforted that the skilled hands of the tailor would make sure it fit me to perfection. I looked at myself in the changing room mirror, my fingers lightly tracing the intricate details of Mom's gown.

I began to feel my heart pound with nervousness and excitement as I stepped out to show my Dad how it looked. He stood beside me and looked at me in the mirror, beaming with pride and trying to hide the tears glistening in his eyes.

"My little girl," he whispered, choking back emotions. "You look so much like your mother. She would have been so proud of the woman you've become."

I hugged him tightly. I had only gotten to know her briefly, but Dad had loved her for most of his lifetime. The stories and memories he shared helped fill in the gaps in understanding the woman we had lost all too soon.

I slipped back into the changing room and took a moment to gather myself before switching back into my clothes and meeting Dad in the waiting area. The good news, because the alterations were so minor, they promised the dress would be ready by the morning.

While we waited for the alterations, Dad and I took a trip to the National Aquarium. We didn't have too much to say. I think we were both a bit overwhelmed at how fast everything was changing. In May I was a high school student. Then I got engaged and graduated before the month was up. By June I was in Summer School courses across the country. Then came August and all of the sudden my identity shifted from being a first year college student to a Mom. Here we were trying to sift through it all. That's a lot of change in 90 days. Dad looked like he had a lot to say, but all that came out was, "I'm so proud of you. So very proud of you."

Jackson's flight arrived and the plan was for him to meet us at the hotel on the harbor where Dad was staying for the weekend. Dad was upstairs resting in his room, a bit emotionally worn by the events of the day, and probably the weekend in general. I hung out in the lobby, caressing the same spot of the oversized blue velvet chair while waiting for him to arrive. I kept glancing at the oversized clock on the wall, counting the minutes until I could see Jackson again. The more time that passed, the more worn the spot I was rubbing. When he finally arrived, I could feel his energy before the lobby door opened.

I stood to my feet and smoothed the wrinkles out of my clothing. My nervous energy was all over the place. He scanned the room then locked in on me like a target. I don't remember moving towards him, but that friendly chair was definitely quite a ways behind me when we finally got to hold each other again.

"Marley!" he eagerly bellowed as he dropped his duffle and wrapped me up in his arms. "Is this real?" He asked as his voice choked with emotion.

"I hope so, Jackson!" I snuggled into his arms and listened to the rhythm of his heartbeat. It was strong, and it felt like the soundtrack of my favorite place on earth.

"I hope so too, Sweetheart!" he whispered. "I missed you so much, Marley!" He said, his breath, warm against my ear.

"I don't have enough words to describe how much I missed you," I said as my voice quivered. He brushed away a tear that escaped from my eye.

"Can I kiss you, Marley or do I have to wait until the wedding?" He joked.

I tilted my face towards his and opened my eyes. His gaze stirred up all the butterflies in my stomach. I spoke what was on my mind, "I missed these big brown eyes, Jackson."

He whimpered and leaned in for a kiss, placing one hand on the side of my face and the other on my belly. I felt a little dizzy and I wasn't sure if it was the kiss or the child. Either way, I took a few steps back to catch my breath and right my steps.

Jax was so excited that he didn't seem to notice I was off balance. "I can't wait to meet whoever this is in here!" He said with tears in his eyes before getting down on one knee to place his face on my stomach next to the baby. That is a memory I'll hold on to forever. Watching him love on our child who wasn't even here yet made my heart leap.

We took his bag up to the room. With Dad sleeping, we decided to go for a walk, hand in hand, along the harbor. We didn't say a word the entire walk but our glances told a story all their own. I knew he was excited to see me. I was overwhelmed with gratitude for the moment and teared up at the horizon that I could see so clearly. Life was in the process of leading us to something more. More than we would've positioned ourselves for. More than we would've dreamt up. More than we could have imagined and it was so beautiful.

After a couple of hours silently meandering around the cobblestone streets, we sat on a bench near the water's edge. The choppy waves lapping against the docks felt a bit unsettling to me. Then Jackson draped an arm behind me and took in a deep breath that felt like it was full of contentment. He handed me an envelope and told me to, "Open this one in the morning, Sweetheart." I nodded and slipped the letter into my pocket, trading it for an envelope with a letter for him to read in the morning.

The sun began its bedtime routine as Jackson looked at me, his eyes glistening as his gaze deepened. He was in serious thought about something but I didn't know what was on his mind.

"What do you think our lives will look like in 20 years, Marley?"

Before I could answer, my phone buzzed strong enough to shake the bond between us. Dad was checking in to see where we were. We met him in the lobby of the hotel and before we could decide where to go for dinner, Jax was reunited with his godparents and his Mom and Dad. We had a quick walkthrough of the wedding on the terrace of the hotel, then settled in for dinner.

I was nervous about meeting Jackson's parents, especially given the unconventional circumstances of our wedding. But all worry dissipated as soon as I met them. They welcomed me with open arms, understanding the depth of love and commitment their son had for me and embracing me like their own daughter. Their presence brought an air of warmth and acceptance, soothing any lingering nerves that were hanging out in my body.

Sitting at the dinner table, the atmosphere lightened as Mr. Charlie and Dr. Chris, who had played a pivotal role in our love story and had been like family to both of us, cracked jokes and shared heartwarming anecdotes from their memories of us as children. Laughter filled the room, bringing a sense of joy and togetherness to the night. Love and nostalgia was ever present and everyone seemed to be thrilled to join this special occasion. As the dinner ended and everyone headed to their respective hotel rooms for the night, Jackson and I lingered for a while longer on the terrace of the hotel, where we were to be married in less than 24 hours. Our hands wouldn't let go of each other. Our eyes wouldn't stray elsewhere, even to the view of the nearly full moon that was hovering overhead. I yawned one too many times and Jackson ushered me off to bed with a sweet goodnight kiss so I could get some rest.

"Remember to read that letter in the morning, Marley."

"I promise to text you after I read it if you'll do the same."

"Promise."

Jax:

The first thing I did when I woke up on our wedding day was to tear open the envelope that Marley had handed me the day before. I stared at her handwriting first, reflecting on how much it had changed over the years, and still how similar it was. She still dotted her I's with an open circle and interchanged lowercase and small caps within the same word.

Hi Ring Bearer,

As I sit here, pen in hand, I find it hard to express the depth of my emotions on this momentous day. Today, we'll stand side by side, pledging our love and commitment to each other, and I couldn't be more excited to embark on this incredible journey with you.

It feels like just yesterday that we were kids, at your godparents' wedding, oblivious to the future that awaited us. Who would have thought that fate had woven our paths together, and that we would become inseparable?

Through the years, our bond grew stronger with every letter we exchanged. I'll never forget the anticipation of receiving your words on paper, holding each letter close to my heart as if you were right there with me. Those letters became the thread that kept us connected when life took us in different directions. Your words were a lifeline, a constant reminder of the love we shared.

There's something magical about the way we fell in love. It wasn't a single grand gesture, but a bunch of shared moments, laughter, tears, dreams, and vulnerabilities that brought us closer. It was in those letters where we bared our souls, sharing our hopes, fears, and aspirations without judgment or reservation. It's a love that has grown and evolved over time, anchored in the foundation of true friendship. I love and appreciate every second of time we've spent together.

Today, as I walk down the aisle towards you, my heart will be filled with overwhelming joy and gratitude. Gratitude for the love we've shared, the memories we've created, and the little miracle growing inside me, a testament to our love and the beginning of our family.

I promise to stand by your side through all of life's twists and turns, to cherish and adore you as we continue to grow together. With you, I've found a love that feels like home, and I know that no matter what life throws at us, we'll face it as a team, supporting and lifting each other higher.

You are my anchor, my safe haven, and my greatest love. I feel so blessed to have you as my partner for life, and I am thrilled to become your wife.

With all the love in my heart,

Marley

Sheesh! How do you focus on anything else when you receive a letter like that on your wedding day? I wiped my eyes free enough from the tears so that I could see my phone and sent her a quick text.

"Good morning future Mrs. Williamson. Your letter was the perfect way to start my day. I'll see you soon!"

She replied with only a smiling emoji which told me that she hadn't yet read my letter.

The morning sun cast a warm glow over the hotel suite as I got up to meet my Mom and Godmother for breakfast. The two of them gushed over how much I'd grown up and the type of man I was becoming. Their focus was on helping me manage my feelings - you know the racing heart filled with a mix of apprehension and excitement.

The majority of the day I spent with my Dad and Godfather, just hanging out in the room and waiting for go time. They had a good time reminiscing about the good ole days, back when they were young and dumb and just learning what it meant to be married. I got all sorts of advice from them.

"Today is a big day, my boy," Mr. Charlie chirped. "You're about to start a beautiful journey with your bride. You remember all those lessons you requested?"

Lola was the reason I initially started asked for tips on how to treat a wife. Then came Marley and her bright light. Everything I learned, everything I asked about was for her.

"I remember," I told him, my hands fidgeting with each other. I didn't know what to do with all that nervous energy and Dad picked up on it.

He chuckled softly and placed a reassuring hand on my shoulder, "It's normal to feel a bit nervous, Jax. Marriage is a big step in life and you're entering into it faster than you expected, I'm sure."

I nodded, grateful to be seen and understood without having to try to explain the mix of emotions that was rolling around within me.

Dad continued, "Marriage is not a destination, son. It's a journey that you'll take with Marley. There will be good times and tough ones, highs and lows, but what matters most is that you face them together. You're on the same team. Listen to your teammate. See what she needs. Tell her your needs and be patient with each other. You're learning a new way to communicate with someone and so is she. It will take time to learn this new version of Marley."

Mr. Charlie nodded in agreement. "Your Dad's right, Jax. Marriage is a team effort. You're not just two individuals sharing a life. You're also a united force, stronger together than apart. Always cherish and respect each other's dreams and goals. Be each other's cheerleader and encouragement."

Hearing their advice brought a sense of peace. A wave of calm washed over me as I soaked up the moment, thanking them both for their thoughts.

"Remember," Mr. Charlie continued, "the small things add up to big things. Those thoughtful gestures let her know that you still see her, and you still choose her. Surprise her. Make her laugh. Never stop dating her."

I gulped down their last bits of wisdom, "You've seen me and Marley grow up together. You're the reason we've been able to connect on a deeper level like this. Your love and support mean the world to me - to both of us."

"Look at that," Dad chirped, "he's already thinking like a team."

My Godfather patted me on my back, "We have no doubt that the two of you are meant to be. I couldn't be more proud of the man you've become, Jackson."

I loved those two before that day, but after pouring into me the way they did, my sense of confidence increased. I was ready to take on the world and face life's challenges and joys with Marley. I noticed the time on the clock and sprang to my feet to get dressed. When I returned, the two of them made a big deal about my tux. Dad straightened up my bowtie and Mr. Charlie took some quick pictures with his phone and sent them to his wife.

I was ready for whatever was next and I sent peaceful energy Marley's way, hoping the same for her.

Marley:

I had woken up when the sun started to peek into the room - its warm orange hue, coloring nearly everything it touched. I was holding onto the sealed envelope from Jackson when I received his text about my letter. I wanted to tell him that I was savoring this last letter as a single woman but that felt too over the top. So instead I just continued to lean into those feelings as they happened, holding them close to my chest and feeling the nostalgia in the moment. The world was still. Dad was sleep. The letter in my hand was all the proof I needed that this decision was the right one. It didn't matter what was in the letter, just the fact that it existed, that he had thought enough in advance to write a letter for me to read, that was all that I needed for reassurance that Jackson and I were going to be okay, regardless of what we faced.

I opened it and the tears started flowing on line one.

Good morning, Marley!

In my head we got married on the same day as my godparents, but today it's the real thing. I can't believe our big day is here. I know it's coming a little faster than we had planned but I'm ridiculously excited to stand there with you, looking all gorgeous in your dress. You're gonna be a knockout, no doubt about it.

You know, I've been thinking about all the crazy stuff we've been through since we met at my godparents' wedding when we were just kids. I have loved you since we were 8 years old. I know that sounds crazy, but it's the truth. When I saw you at that wedding, I just wanted to be close to you. Your light and your energy are like a magnet - a beacon for me; drawing me near and calling me home. I'm so excited to feel it again.

Those letters we wrote? Man, they were like our secret little world. Sharing our hopes, dreams, and even our fears without holding back—it made me feel so connected to you, even when we were apart. It's like we've got this unique bond that no one else can understand, and it's pretty damn amazing.

I want you to know that you mean everything

to me, Marley. You're not just my girl; you're my best friend, my confidante, and now, you're gonna be the mother of our child. Can you believe it? I can't wait to see you as a mom, and I promise to be the best dad I can be too.

When I see you walking down that aisle, I know I'm gonna be a hot mess, trying not to bawl my eyes out. But hey, it's all happy tears, alright? I'll be standing there, thinking about how lucky I am to have you by my side. And when we say our vows, I'll mean every word with all my heart. I can't wait to build the beautiful life we wrote about in our superhero story.

Life's gonna throw some crazy stuff our way, but I know we can handle it together. We got this, Marley, and I can't wait to tackle all the adventures that lie ahead, side by side.

I'm counting down the hours until I get to call you my wife. Until then, just know that I love you like crazy, and I always will.

See you at the altar, sweetheart.

Yours forever,
Jackson

I grabbed a tissue and blotted my eyes and nose then picked up my phone. "Our story begins soon, Awkward Man. Love you lots!"

He replied with the kissing face emoji and I took in a deep cleansing breath. There was a knock on the door of our suite. Mom's dress had been delivered and just the sight of it brought more tears than I was ready to part with. The knock had startled Dad awake and we took a moment to say a quick prayer of gratitude for the day that we were given. He had ordered room service waffles for breakfast and I was in hog heaven. The two of us ate and talked about the news of the day - not the wedding, the literal news. I think Dad was a bit more overwhelmed than I was. That was his distraction.

When it was time to get dressed, I found myself surrounded by Jackson's family in the hotel suite. The excitement in the room was palpable, and the anticipation of the upcoming ceremony filled the air. My heart was both heavy and elated as I prepared to put on my late mother's gown. Mrs. Williamson, and Dr. Chris stood by my side, ready to assist in the sacred ritual of getting dressed.

Dr. Chris' eyes glistened with emotion as she held my hands in hers. "You look so much like your mother, Marley. She would have been so proud of the woman you've become," she said - her voice filled with affection and love.

Mrs. Williamson stepped forward, holding a delicate pearl necklace that had belonged to her own mother. "My mom wore this on her wedding day, as did I, Marley. I thought it would be a beautiful way to carry on the tradition and fill it with new memories," she said, gently placing it around my neck.

Tears welled up in my eyes as I touched the pearls, feeling the weight of their family's presence in that simple and meaningful gesture. I hugged her tightly, sharing my gratitude for the support and love that she and Dr. Chris had showered upon me.

With a tender smile, Mrs. Williamson nodded and said, "Now let's get you into this beautiful dress so you can go get married to your best friend."

Carefully, they helped me step into the gown, adjusting the lace and buttons with meticulous care. The dress fit me perfectly, as though it had been waiting for this very moment. As they fastened the buttons along the back, I felt an overwhelming sense of connection to my mom and the love she had shared with my Dad.

Dr. Chris handed me a delicate lace veil, one that had been carefully preserved over the years. "Your father told me that your mom wore this same veil on her wedding day. He said that it, and this dress, are symbols of love that transcends time, generations, and astral planes."

As she placed the veil upon my head, I could feel the love and support from my new family, welcoming me in with open arms. Mrs. Williamson hugged me tightly and my heart felt lighter, knowing I had the support of Jackson's family, who in this one simple moment had become my family too. Because of their help, I was ready to walk down the aisle in my mother's gown and veil, carrying the legacy of love and strength she had poured into me before she left us.

CHAPTER NINE
LOVE'S SUNSET
AGE 18

Marley:

Before they let in the guests, they quietly whisked me up to a closet on the rooftop terrace of the hotel. It had been transformed into a magical setting for the wedding. Strings of twinkling fairy lights adorned the railings, casting a soft glow over the entire area. Elegant floral arrangements in shades of ivory, blush, and deep crimson adorned the tables, adding a touch of romance to the scene. I don't know how they pulled all of that off so quickly, but it was breathtaking.

Soft jazz music played in the background, creating an atmosphere of sophistication and charm.

At the center of the terrace stood a beautifully decorated arch, entwined with vines and fresh flowers. It symbolized our journey of growth and love, from childhood friends to soulmates. Underneath the arch was a rustic wooden altar, where we would exchange our vows.

The sunset painted the sky with hues of orange, pink, and purple, creating a breathtaking backdrop for the ceremony. The moment approached and anticipation grew, as evidenced by the soft murmur of excitement that filled the air.

As the music changed, signaling the beginning of the ceremony, the guests stood up, and the doors of the closet opened. My dad winked at me and proudly walked me down the aisle. Tears welled up in his eyes as he gave me away to Jackson, who stood at the end of the aisle, beaming at me.

The officiant, a close family friend, spoke eloquently about love, destiny, and the beauty of finding it in unexpected places. She shared heartwarming stories of how the two of us had connected at a young age at our godparents wedding and had kept our love alive through letters and memories.

Our heartfelt vows rooted me in the promise of all that could be as we pledged to cherish and support each other through all of life's challenges and triumphs. The love and devotion in Jackson's words were evident, and everyone in attendance seemed to be captivated by the depth of our emotions.

After exchanging rings and sealing our promises with a passionate kiss, we walked back down the aisle hand in hand, our smiles shining brighter than the stars that would soon grace the night sky.

As the evening progressed, the reception area was revealed to be a chic and stylish space adorned with white and gold accents. The head table featured a stunning floral centerpiece that cascaded down its length, creating a romantic focal point.

We shared our first dance as husband and wife, moving gracefully to a timeless love song that held special meaning for us. The dance floor soon filled with family and friends, all there to celebrate the joyous occasion.

To honor my mother, a table was set up with photographs and mementos, allowing everyone to feel her presence and remember the woman who had played such an important role in my life.

During the heartfelt speeches, there was laughter, tears, and endless applause. Family and friends shared touching anecdotes, celebrating our love and wishing us a lifetime of happiness.

As the night drew to a close, a sweet dessert table was unveiled, offering an array of decadent treats, including a cake adorned with delicate sugar flowers. The aroma of coffee and hot cider with sugarplums filled the air, inviting guests to savor the moment and indulge in the sweetness of the evening.

We found ourselves surrounded by loved ones, feeling grateful for the support and love that enveloped us. It had been a day filled with emotions, memories, and the promise of a bright future together.

Hand in hand, our fingers interlaced, we made our way to a private corner of the terrace, stealing a few quiet moments to cherish our newlywed bliss. The stars twinkled overhead, a beautiful symbol of the eternal love we had found in each other. With a heart full of love and dreams, I looked forward to the journey that lay ahead—a journey that began with a chance meeting at a wedding and blossomed into a love that would endure for a lifetime.

Contrast that wedding night with what was a travel

day for everyone but me and you almost couldn't get much more opposing emotions.

I had a sinking feeling as I took my husband to the airport that something major was on the way. I didn't think it was the child I was carrying, but I knew in my gut that it was going to change things for us - and it didn't feel like that change was going to be a positive one. I didn't mention it to anyone else. I ate that feeling and digested it, hoping it would pass sooner than later and I'd forget that it was even something that crossed my path. We held onto each other for as long as we could - soaking up the feeling of each other's bodies, the scent of each other's skin, the waves of emotion we could feel in each other's eyes.

That was the last time I saw Jackson for a while. Far longer than we had planned anyway. Though I had felt something brewing, in that moment I was blissfully unaware of the curveball that life had in store for us.

Dear Jackson,

I don't know how to reach you by phone so I have to send this in a letter and I'm terribly sorry that you're finding out like this. I just got discharged from the hospital. It's only been a few days since you left Baltimore, but I got into an accident on my way back to the residence halls after taking Dad to the airport the same night I took you there. I didn't break any bones and I only have a few minor bruises, but my heart is broken.

The baby I was carrying, our child, did not survive the accident. The doctors said the blunt force trauma was too much for the baby's tiny body. I thought we were okay. I got a ride back to the residence hall after the emts checked me out at the site of the accident. I got to sleep for part of that night and then the most excruciating feeling came as I was laying in bed. I couldn't get up and I didn't know what was happening. I went into shock and my RA called for the campus police, who called for an ambulance. The relaying of information cost us time that we didn't have.

My one job as a mother was to protect our child, and I know this one wasn't born yet, but I couldn't save them. If I can't protect an unborn child, what kind of mom would I be to one who was alive?

I'm angry at the drunk driver who ran the red-light. I'm angry that the seatbelt which was there to protect me, also did harm to our unborn child. I'm devastated at this loss and I feel guilty that I couldn't protect them and I don't know what this means for us.

I feel like I failed both of us in the biggest way possible, Jackson, and I understand if you want to change your mind about us. You were so excited about what was next and that all looks different now.

I'm so sorry, Jackson.

I love you so much. This is a pain I wish we could navigate together - in person.

Please write me back. I need your arms to be my shelter.

Love you lots,
Marley

CHAPTER TEN
DISTANCE CAN'T DIM LOVE
AGE 23

Marley:

I didn't know what to do with myself. He sent two quick texts while I was on the phone with my stepmom. Not even 30 seconds after I got off the phone with her, my phone rang again. Jackson. I answered the phone, "How can I help you Mr. Williamson?"

"Hey Marley. Did you get my texts? I'm on my way to your house to drop off this card from my godparents. They didn't want me to mail it to you. They said I had to hand deliver it."

"Oh. Wait, you're on the way here?"

"Yes ma'am."

"You haven't been here in at least 5 years. Do you need the address?"

"No I remember how to get to you." Awkward silence hung in the air. "I mean...I still know my way to your house."

"Okay."

"I'll call you when I'm close."

"No need, I'll unlock the door. Just knock before you come inside."

"Yes ma'am." We sat in silence for a few minutes. It seemed that neither of us knew exactly what to say in the moment, but neither of us wanted to go.

"How far away are you?" I asked as I sprang to my feet and unlocked the front door before I forgot.

There was a knock at the door and then as if in slow motion, it opened. The sunlight flooded my view, leaving only a silhouette of a taller, more chiseled figure than I had dropped off at the airport all those years go.

He exhaled when he saw me, and held out the card for me to hold.

I held my hand to my heart - a reminder to breathe. "Hi, Jackson."

He cleared his throat then spoke, "Hi, Marley Mar."

He handed the card to me and I thanked him for bringing it to the house. He nodded, almost as if he were devoid of words, which was the complete opposite of the last time we saw each other. We were two heartbroken, hot-headed, recently divorced teenagers without a filter - a dangerous combination. I assumed he would hate me forever.

At least 30 seconds passed as we stood there in silence, gazing at each other. His face had matured, and his frame stood straight as a board. There was still sorrow in his eyes though. Uncertain of how else to respond, I smiled reassuredly in his direction. He nodded and exhaled deeply. He was only in the house for about a minute.

He averted his eyes and blurted, "Welp. I better go."

"Oh. So soon?" I asked him.

He looked up at my face, his eyes frozen on mine. "I'm on my way to the - the...the, umm.." He snapped his fingers as his brain tried to find the words. "I need to go."

I spoke softly, "Okay," and extended my arm to welcome in a hug, if he'd have it.

His eyebrows scrunched together, he nodded as though he were telling himself that it was okay, then opened his arm to fold me in for a side hug. We stood right there in the foyer. We hadn't advanced into the house any further than that. The two of us, one arm wrapped around each other. Instinctively, my head dropped onto his shoulder and almost as if it were a reflex, his head dropped onto the top of mine. That was my safe place. That was home.

I squeezed his waist like I was trying to wring water from a sponge and let the love pour out of me. I missed him. His arms. His presence. His scent. His essence. I soaked it all in. I held on for as long as I could - for as long as he would let me. Then when I tried to ease up to be courteous of his space, I felt it. His squeeze and that deep and lingering sigh of contentment brought back the butterflies. It almost felt as if he missed me too.

In a near whisper, I spoke, "I appreciate you, Jackson." I let go of my grasp and instead let my hand drop.

He stood upright, his hand no longer holding in the curves of my more mature body. "Thank you. I appreciate you too, Marley," he said before cracking a joke on his way out the door.

Once I got to know the real him in high school, Jackson had brought out the softer side of me. We were five years removed from that but I could still let down my guard around him. In that moment, it felt like anything was possible. In that moment, I had a fleeting thought that our love could still thrive. The spark was there, in his eyes, in the space between us, in his hug, in the hurried way he left the house, in the text he sent me from the car before he drove away.

"Wow. I didn't expect to feel that again."

Jax:

I felt like I had been set up. My godparents knew where she lived but they waited until I was back in the city before asking me to deliver Marley's graduation card to her. I didn't know why I was so nervous but it was hard to find air to breathe. Every time I inhaled it felt like my lungs were already near capacity. So short wimpy breaths it was.

I called her after sending texts that I wasn't sure made sense. I knew it was a risk, given what happened the last time we talked, but it was a risk that I had to take - for my godparents sake I mean. I thought I was gonna leave a message, but she answered the phone and caught me off guard. The air was even lighter than before. Breathing had become so much of a problem that I knew I needed to keep the convo short. So I hopped off the phone as fast as I'd hopped on it.

She asked if I knew the way to her house. I'd spent the entire summer after graduation, at her house, well - what we had of that summer anyway. I always thought we'd have more time, but we just didn't. And that didn't bode well for us. I didn't know how to miss her without taking it out on her. I didn't understand how to love her through the pain of separation. All I knew is I was miserable without her. At least, that's what I thought at the time. The truth is, I was miserable with the choices I made and I used our relationship as a cover for my misery. I was mad that I wasn't going to be with Marley. I loved her so much, but

I was too angry with myself to be anything good for her, for us. I said some dumb stuff. I did some dumb stuff, and Marley just tried to understand what was happening. It all melted away like a snowman in a house in the dead of winter. Our relationship, hell - our friendship, turned into a puddle of water on the kitchen floor, quick, fast, and in a hurry.

You could kind of see it building in our old letters. So yes, I was surprised that she answered my call - then I wondered if she would have answered all those years ago. I pulled up in front of her house while we were still on the phone. She had asked me to knock before I came inside. So I did, and she was standing right there in the entryway.

Her face still glowed, and that light was still very much alive within her. *Steel yourself, Jackson. Steel yourself.* She was the only person I'd met up to that point who had such a physical impact on me. She literally took my breath away. I fought to remind myself why I was there and I stuck the card straight out in front of me. We exchanged greetings and then nothing. I just stared at her and she stared back at me. It was like neither of us knew what to say. It reminded me of the way we left things after we last saw each other - in silence, without saying a word. I started to get an uneasy feeling in my gut as I thought about it. I wanted to preserve this meeting. It was good. I could end things on a good note, so I tried to leave, but she wouldn't let me without giving me a hug.

I loved the way her head rested on my shoulder. My head was drawn to hers. Hell, I was drawn to her. I just held on and squeezed the way I had wanted to so many times in the five years leading up to that hug. She was like a security blanket for me. Had me out there like Linus and blue. I wanted to stay in that forever. I wanted to love her forever. I wondered if she'd still have me. It was pure torture. I missed that. I missed us. I didn't know there was as much air in my body as what escaped when she let go of her grasp.

I wanted to say so much. But I wanted to keep this meeting positive. I still loved her. I don't know if she could feel it, but I definitely still loved her. She'll always be my girl. I rushed out the door in a hurry. My brain was overwhelmed with it all. It rushed in like a flood. I had to escape.

So I did - as fast as I could. Then I sent her a text.

"Wow. I didn't expect to feel that again."

She replied almost immediately, "What did you feel Jackson?"

"Can we talk about it over coffee someday soon?"

"I think I'd like that."

"I'll text you again when I get somewhere safe."

"Okay be careful."

That's what she used to say when she was mad at me. Be careful. It was her way of letting me know that she still loved me even when she wasn't happy with me right then. My brain was trying to find a balance between over processing the situation and staying calm. But my word she was still the most beautiful person I knew. It's not that I was expecting the opposite, but time had been REALLY good to her. The curves were curving. Her hair smelled amazing and it's not like she knew I was coming to see her on that day. I kind of just sprung it on her. From no contact to hey I'm at your house. She didn't even have time to change because I was basically at her door before we got off the phone. So what I saw really was representative of what I'd get. The inner beauty was still freakin' radiant. The outer beauty was - well, let's just say she was a show stopper. She made overalls and a t-shirt look good. It only took a minute, literally 60 seconds, but I was hooked again.

Anyway, I texted her back, "Will do." Then drove safely - you know, slowly, back to my apartment. She replied with a smiling face emoji but I didn't see it until I climbed the nine flights of steps to the top floor of the building, let myself in my apartment, then sat down on my couch.

"Safely in my apartment. Send me some options for lunch. What times work for you?"

"OOooo...you're in an apartment now. I thought you said coffee lol - M,W,F noon - 1:00."

"I am and I did. You have a preference on the day?"

"All three...just kidding."

"How about tomorrow, Monday."

"Sure, that works for me."

"The Combine? Noon. I can pick you up or we can meet there. I'll yield to your comfort level."

"I'm comfortable with you picking me up. But you'll have to get me from work instead of my house."

"Cool. Drop me an address and I'll text you when I'm about 5 minutes away."

"I'm interning at Hope Gardens this summer."

As SOON as I read her reply it was confirmation that we had been set up. There was no way ON EARTH that Marley could have been interning at the same hospital where my godmother worked and she not know about it. She could've given Marley the card without needing me to hand deliver it. But because she didn't, there I was sitting on my couch sifting through those old feelings again. Dr. Chris was added to my hit list.

I texted Marley back.

"I didn't know that. I'll see you tomorrow at noon." She

didn't send any words to me in return, but she did drop a heart on the message. Then she changed it to a thumbs up. I spent the next hour trying to decipher what that meant before I finally just let it go.

When Monday came I sent her a message, "Good morning. Still feel up to connecting today?"

"Good morning! Yep."

"Good. I'll see you soon."

"Anxiously awaiting it." That sent me.

She could've replied with any combination of words, but that she was honest in how she was feeling meant a lot to me and instead of doing what I used to do in the past, I told her how it felt.

"That just made my heart flutter."

"Just trying to be honest, Jackson."

"I appreciate it Marley. Me too. I'll be there at 11:55 so you won't have to wait on me." She dropped a heart emoji on that reply and I waited for it to change. It never did.

I shot her a text at 11:50 that I was about 5 minutes away from the hospital. Then at 11:55, when I pulled up to find a parking spot, she walked out the double doors and headed straight across the drive towards my car. I put it in park and rushed to get out and open the door before she could open it herself.

She hugged me tightly. I swear she had to know what she did to me. I froze momentarily. It was like my brain had stopped. I just held on and dropped my face onto her head until she let go and hopped in the car. I closed the door and held her gaze as I walked in front of the car on the way to the driver's door. I was feeling all the feels. Dr. Chris was On. My. List.

I got in the car and Marley was all smiles. The Combine was only a couple of minutes away, so we didn't say much in the car. Just the normal, "How's your day going?" conversation.

When I helped her out of the car at the restaurant, she reached for my hand. Her touch was still electric. She had the force of a magnet, drawing me in without any fight. It was like I had to submit to the will of the energy. That was something I fought against 5 years before, but that fight got us no where. So this time I gave in and flowed with it. I held her hand as we walked towards the door. She had me - all over again.

We were seated near a window and I couldn't look at anything, anyone except her. We just stared at each other and smiled until the waiter came and asked for our drink orders. When he left I joked that we should probably figure out what we're eating before he came back.

When he returned with our drinks and asked for our order we were ready. When he left again, Marley jumped right into the deep end. No wading in the shallow bits. Let's get straight to the nitty gritty, kid.

"So what did you feel yesterday, Jackson?"

I smiled at how brash she was. "Shit. So we're not gonna ease into this conversation at all?"

"What's the point of easing in? We both know that we're gonna talk about it today. So let's talk!"

I wiped the condensation off my glass of water, I think it was a way to soothe the sweat beading up on my own brow. I could feel it bubbling up to the surface.

"Okay, let's talk about it. I'm sorry for how I acted 5 years ago. I was a dumb hurt, kid, and you got caught in my stuff."

"Is that what you felt yesterday?"

"Yeah, part of it. After I got home anyway. But those 60 seconds at your house..."

"Yeah?"

"Every ounce of love that I've been storing up for the last 5 years just resurfaced in an instant when you opened the door. I didn't even know I was storing it up until I saw your face."

"Jackson"

"Then it all came rushing back to the surface."

"Are you being serious right now?"

"Why? What's so hard to believe about what I'm saying? Is it the -"

"I just want to make sure before I tell you that I felt the same thing."

I stared at her to make sure she wasn't kidding around. My heart was beating through my chest. She reached across the table for my hand and quietly asked me to breathe with her. I didn't realize I had stopped, but I guess I shouldn't have been surprised. That was a common occurrence for the two of us. I slid my fingers between hers and we sat in silence, looking longingly into the depths of each others souls - until the pizza arrived, and we were snapped back into the present moment.

"That kinda felt like we were in a different dimension."

"I'm glad you said it!" I told her between chuckles. "I was thinking, 'don't say that out loud, she'll think you're crazy.'"

"I mean I already know you're crazy, so..."

She got me. I mean really understood me. My girl.

Marley:

Jax had been working on his honesty. Things he used to keep to himself, he let roll off the tongue. We talked about whatever came to mind at that lunch. It almost felt like we were purging all of our pent up emotions and thoughts. When I told him that I missed him, he sat beside me in the booth. Our waiter came back to check on us and nodded in respect when he saw Jax with his arm around my shoulder. It was like our soul deflating split had never happened.

He made sure that I made it back to work early. With some of the extra time, the two of us sat in his car trying to figure out what was next for us. We had gone from married, to divorced and not speaking, to whatever it was we were feeling in the moment. He had the look in his eye. I knew what was about to come out of his mouth.

His words, so softly spoken. Almost a whisper, "Can I kiss you?"

"On our date."

"Okay. On our date," he grinned. "What time am I picking you up?"

"Tomorrow at 6."

"Tomorrow? 6pm?"

"Yes tomorrow, but 6am. Are you available?"

"I'll make time for you, Marley. I'm guessing you have something specific in mind?"

"I do."

"And you're not going to tell me. Alright."

"I need to get back to work, Jackson. I'll text you when I'm off. Okay?" I leaned in and kissed him on the cheek. He nodded and touched his face with the back of his hand.

"I'll pick you up bright and early tomorrow."

It came out before I could stop it, "Okay. I love you, Jackson."

A huge grin spread across his face as he sat back against the driver's side door, his right hand covering his heart - seemingly in disbelief, "I love you too, Marley."

I hopped out of the car and bopped through the doors of the hospital entrance with an extra spring in my step. When I turned around, he was still watching, waving with the hand that wasn't holding his heart in his chest.

CHAPTER ELEVEN
A SUNRISE REUNION
AGE 23

Marley:

The next morning, I was up bright and early and checked to see if he had received my text from the night before. I had asked him to dress in clothes he was okay getting a little dirt on and not to come ring the doorbell or knock on the door. He replied not long after I sent my message but I was exhausted from a long day at Hope Gardens and my phone was on do not disturb while I was busy catching up on my beauty rest.

"Yes ma'am. What are we about to get into?"

I slipped on some jogging pants and tennies, then threw on one of his old t-shirts from his high school days and replied to it that morning. "Hey, sorry! Long days mean early nights. We're going outside. Hope I'll see you soon!"

I stood at the front window, watching anxiously for his car to arrive in the driveway. Things happened so quickly the other day that I didn't have time to experience all the anxious build up that comes with seeing someone special again for the first time in 5 years. Now that we had lunch and the awkward first real conversation out of the way, I felt like I had been transported back to high school. Dawn was beginning to break and the birds were starting to chirp their melodic morning songs. My heart was racing with a mix of anticipation and nervousness. I couldn't believe that I was about to kiss my ex-husband again.

He slowly pulled into the driveway. I threw on a hoodie and quietly slipped out of the house so I wouldn't wake Dad. Jackson was waiting for me outside of his car. His face when I stepped outside, it was always the same - this look of amazement and pure love and it made me smile. He hugged me and his voice rumbled "Well...Good Morning, Marley. Don't you look cute!"

I whispered my good morning in his ear and felt every inch of his embrace, holding on for as long as I could.

Jax:

I pulled into her driveway, sent her a text to let her know I had arrived and waited outside the car. She didn't want me to ring the doorbell but I could still open her car door. I'm not sure I needed to send the text though because she came outside before I even received the delivered notification. Her hair was back in a fro hawk and the hoodie she was wearing was from grad night. I was instantly taken back to that night and how happy I was to be standing beside her, how ready I was to start our lives together.

Now there she was, back in my life, still as beautiful as ever and so damn cute. My breath caught in my throat, a thousand emotions flooding through me.

"Well...Good Morning, Marley. Don't you look cute!"

She didn't say a word, but the smile that played on her lips told a full story and I was ready to read it cover to cover. Her hug was so tight. She squeezed like we hadn't just seen each other the day before but I welcomed it. There were so many times I needed one of her hugs throughout that 5 year drought that every hug felt like it was worth a million dollars to me. She was making me a wealthy man. Even more so when she whispered good morning into my ear. I apologized for what she was about to feel and she squeezed me tighter so I couldn't wriggle away in shame.

She continued to whisper, "You're up early today."

I chuckled into her ear and somehow she managed to close the microscopic distance between us as she exhaled a contented sigh.

"I'm assuming there's a time sensitive reason we're up this early. Do we need to go?" I asked as I kept her cocooned in my arms and walked her around to the passenger side of the car.

"Mmmm hmmm," she affirmed. I opened the door and told her I had more hugs stored up for her. She let go and our eyes locked. I tilted my head towards the car and motioned for her to get inside.

I trekked back to the driver's side of the car after closing the door, a mix of joy and anticipation surged through my body.

I looked to her for directions.

"Our after prom spot."

To the lake I drove. We found the same cove but it looked different - not worn because of the passing of time, but the break of day felt more promising than the night. I helped her out of the car, not because I thought she needed it, but because that's how Mr. Charlie had taught me to treat a wife.

It was a crisp morning, the air a bit dewy but temperatures in the 50s. "I can't believe there isn't someone already out here fishing."

"I can't either but I'm grateful there isn't, Jax." It was the first time she'd called me Jax since we reunited. We sat down on a fallen log, our fingers gently interlacing. Memories of 5 years ago came flooding back and with it, all the shared secrets and dreams we had whispered to each other on paper. Those were the conversations that had shaped my heart and laid the foundation for the love I was still feeling for Marley.

The first golden rays of dawn began to pierce through the trees on the shoreline opposite where we sat, casting a warm glow on the lake that sat still and tranquil before any eager boaters had disrupted it. Marley leaned into my shoulder and I wrapped an arm around her and softly checked to see if she was okay.

"I'm a little chilly, Jackson." All she had to say was chilly and I was already at the car grabbing my blanket from the back.

"I remember this," she whispered, her voice a delicate mix of glee and uncertainty.

"It's the same guy from prom," I spoke as I carefully wrapped her up in warmth, placing the blanket around her shoulders.

I sat down beside her on the log and she extended her left arm and draped the blanket around my shoulders too. My right hand traced her back from one side to the other as it found a place to rest on her right hip. She scooted closer to me, snuggling into my shoulder again, letting her weight and worries rest on me. That old familiar feeling of warmth, that familiar touch that I thought I had lost forever, both were back. I could feel her heartbeat as it pulsed through her back and beat in sync with mine. I wondered what old memories this had drummed up for her.

Her head still resting on my shoulder, she looked up at me. Those eyes that always pierced my soul, were full of sincerity and longing that morning.

A tear glistened in the corner of her eye as she whispered, "I've missed this so much, Jax." I couldn't get any words to the surface of my mouth. A nod was the best I could do in the moment, so I rested my temple against the top of her head. We sat in silence as the sky began to transform. The horizon was set ablaze with orange and pink, that was mirrored on the surface of the water. It was like Mother Nature was trying to compete for the most beautiful view that morning. Don't get me wrong, that was a beautiful sunrise, but looking down and seeing my love filled with happiness, with hope, with ease and comfort, that was the most beautiful view I could ever see. So that sunrise, as breathtaking as it was, and it was a stunner, was a distant second place on that day.

"It's so beautiful, Jackson."

"You are," I replied.

"I mean the lake, the sky, this moment," she said.

I whispered softly into her ear, "Mmm hmm. All of it, and so are you. This is pretty perfect, Marley. Thank you for this."

"It's almost perfect," she whispered.

"What's missing?" I asked softly. "Say the word and I'll fix it - well, if it's within my power to."

She sat up and turned in my direction, those eyes shimmering with tenderness. In that moment, as the sun broke free from the horizon, she leaned in my direction, tipping her head back slightly and presenting those perfect lips of hers to me.

I nodded and squeezed her hip, leaning down towards her to let her know that I got the memo. Our lips met softly, a gentle caress filled with years of longing and unspoken words. It was a kiss of forgiveness and second chances. It was full of the promise of a future yet to be written.

Our souls had wrapped around each other again, so much in fact that I had a hard time figuring out where hers ended and mine began. That sunrise date was probably the best way for us to rekindle the love that had been dormant for so long. The stillness of the morning brought with it a peaceful serenity - one that felt symbolic, like our journey had just begun to reclaim the love that we let slip away. I knew it would take work to build a future where our hearts could dwell forever. But it was work that was well worth the labor to me.

We continued to sit in silence for awhile and watched the sun ascend higher in the sky - casting its warmth upon our faces. Marley broke that silence with a giggle out of nowhere.

"What's so funny?" I asked her.

"I just realized that I didn't get to finish answering your question."

Confused, I asked for her help, "Which question?"

"What's missing?"

"Was that not what was missing?" I asked as she giggled some more and shook her head in dissent. "Oh no. I jumped the gun."

"No, I wanted that too," she said - that glimmer still in

her eyes.

"So what's missing, Marley? I want this date to be..." I couldn't finish my thought because she leaned in and kissed me again. You know one thing I learned in that moment that was still present from high school? When I initiated the kiss, I felt more in control of my emotions. When she surprised me with one, I got all spring feverish inside. Slightly out of control, and I liked it. A lot. So much so, I almost fell off the log as she broke from our embrace and answered my question.

"Waffles."

I couldn't control my outburst of laughter, so I kissed her softly on the crown of her head and stood up, helping her to her feet as well. I leaned in for one quick kiss before whispering into her ear, "C'mon. Let's go get you some waffles, Mar - before we make a baby out here."

"You mean another one?" She stated matter of factly. Her hand instinctively covered her womb. Her eyes bore a hole into mine.

I felt all the blood drain from my face. Time was at a standstill. The breeze disappeared and in the moment, it felt like it took all of my oxygen with it.

"Yes. I'm so sorry sweetheart. I didn't mean it like -" I paused, knowing there was no way for me to reverse engineer the words that had so haphazardly flown out of my mouth, and nothing I could say to take away the pain that was still present.

She nodded. Her eyes instantly filled with tears. Her soft voice trembled, "Waffles can wait."

I scooped her up in my arms right there where we stood. The tears that filled her eyes soaked through my shirt and I cried with her. I don't know how long we stood out there in nature - birds chirping, fish breaking in the water that had begun to lap against the shoreline - listening to life all around us, helping each other grieve. I only know, this was the embrace that was long overdue.

CHAPTER TWELVE
SEPARATION & HEARTBREAK
AGE 23

Marley:

We stood outside, holding each other's heart during the sunrise until my stomach made itself known. Then Jax asked me if I still wanted waffles. He was so tender with me. So gentle. His eyes, a mix of sorrow and hope. This was what I needed 5 years earlier. This was who I needed him to be 5 years before, but that situation was all too much for us at such a young age. We weren't ready. I wasn't ready. We struggled. It broke us like a shattered plate. We tried to put the pieces back together but some parts were missing and there were holes too large to make it functional in its original form. That, I think, is where we went wrong.

We tried to make our marriage whole like it was before

the plate broke. We didn't understand that the plate had to be different now, that there would always be small pieces we'd discover down the road that no longer fit into the form of the plate because we had pieced it back together without those shards. Pieces that would remind us of when the plate initially broke and remind us of the shattering all over again. No. Instead we got mad that we couldn't eat off of a broken plate and we lashed out at each other along the way.

The letters we had written to each other during that time were shards of the plate that I'd re-read to from time to time because they helped me understand what we had experienced on a deeper level. They were always heartbreaking to read, but it didn't stop me from reading them. I always felt stronger on the other side of the break.

Good Morning Marley,

I hope this letter finds you well, my love. I miss you more than words can express. It's hard to believe we're separated by a thousand miles during this difficult time. I want you to know that you're constantly in my thoughts, especially as we navigate through the pain of our recent loss. Please remember that we're in this together, no matter the distance.

I wish I could be there to hold you and comfort you during these moments of grief. I know it's tough, but let's lean on our love and support each other as we heal. Remember, we're a team, and we can get through anything together.

Sending all my love and strength your way.

Yours forever,
Ring Bearer

Hi Ring Bearer,

Your words brought tears to my eyes. Good tears versus the tears of sadness I've been encountering.

Thank you for your unwavering support, even from afar. It's comforting to know that you're thinking of me during this trying time. I wish you were here, holding my hand, as we navigate this painful journey together.

I must admit, though, that sometimes the distance feels unbearable. The nights are long, and the emptiness weighs heavily on my heart. But your love gives me hope and the strength to keep going. Let's continue to be there for each other, even if we can't physically be together.

Love you lots,
Marley

Good Morning Marley,

I understand the pain you're going through, and I want more than anything to be by your side. I wish there was something more I could do to lessen your pain. Please know that you're not alone in this journey. Lean on our love, and don't hesitate to reach out whenever you need someone to talk to.

I can sense a change in your words, my love, and I worry about the toll this loss is taking on us. Remember, we're in this together. Let's keep communicating openly, even when it's difficult, and find solace in each other's arms, no matter the distance.

With all my love,
Your Groom

My Groom,

I appreciate your concern and your efforts to comfort me, but lately, I've been feeling so disconnected. It's been weeks since we lost the baby and I'm still struggling like it just happened. This loss has shaken me to my core, and it's difficult to find solace even in our love.

I feel so alone and it's hard to see a way forward. I thought we would grow stronger together through this pain, but sometimes it feels like we're drifting apart. Your absence magnifies the emptiness I feel inside. I don't blame you for not being here physically, but sometimes it's hard not to resent it.

I don't want to lose what we have, but I need you to understand how fragile I feel right now. We need to find a way to bridge this gap between us and rediscover the love that bound us together and created the miracle that once lived within me.

Love you lots,
Marley

Marley,

Good Morning.

Your words break my heart. I didn't realize how big of an emotional strain this would place on you. I'm sorry I've failed to be there for you as I should have. I can't wait until they give us our tech back. I need to see your face. I need you to see mine so you understand it's okay. It's all going to be okay. I love you. I choose you.

I'm only away for us, just until this training is done and then I'll be able to move where you are. This feels big, and it is, Marley. But it's short term. Please don't give in to the resentment.

Let's seek help to guide us through this challenging time. Our love is worth fighting for, and I know we can rebuild what has been damaged.

Always yours,
Jax

Jax,

I appreciate your willingness to seek help, but the distance between us feels insurmountable. The pain of our loss has revealed a gulf that I'm not sure we can bridge. Perhaps it's time for us to confront the reality that our love may not be enough to overcome the challenges we're facing.

Please know that my decision isn't made lightly. It's born out of the realization that we both deserve happiness, even if it means finding it apart from each other.

With a heavy heart and lots of love,
Marley

Marley,

Your words hit me like a mack truck. I never thought that our journey through grief would lead us here. It pains me to acknowledge that my love may not be enough to heal the wounds we carry. I know that a lot of time has passed between our letters. I've been trying to find the right words to say but know that I'm fighting for us. I need you to fight for us.

Why won't you fight for us?

If this is truly what you want, I will respect your decision, but I don't think it's really what you want. Is it?

Know that my love for you will never fade, even if we don't make it. I will always remember your beautiful face, your kind heart, and every memory we shared.

Write me back,
Jax

Jackson,

As I write this, tears are streaming down my face. It breaks my heart to see the love we once shared slipping away.

I do fight. Every single day. But you're not here and I am - in the room where it happened. So every day that I wake up, I remember it. It lives within me the way that your love does, but this takes up so much more room - and it's so heavy that it's breaking the floors. It's a mercilessly potent concoction of sadness and shame, of guilt and grief, of worry, and of remorse for wanting to breathe freely again. Every. Single. Day. And I fight until it's time to go back to sleep and dream - the only place where I catch a break, the only place I feel your comfort.

Dad visits every now and then and I always hope you've tagged along with him to surprise me and wrap me up in the safety of your arms. But it's only ever him. Just him. I need more than words, Jackson. Love is holding each other through grief. I need YOU more now than I think I ever have in my life, Ring Bearer. I don't want to let go of what we had, but the pain of holding on feels unbearable, unconquerable even.

Let's take some time apart to heal and rediscover ourselves. Maybe, in time, we'll find a way back to each other. Please know that you'll always have a special place in my heart, in a space where nobody else will have access.

With love,
Marley

Marley,

I hate this. ALL OF IT!!! Love is a choice.

You're my wife. You always will be. Nobody can change that. Not the pieces of paper you sent with the last letter. Not the person who legally nullifies our marriage. Nobody.

I understand your need for space, and hope this time apart will bring clarity and peace to you. If fate permits, I still hope for a future where our paths cross again and our family, however it looks, will bloom.

Always in my thoughts. Always my girl.

I'll love you forever,
Jackson

p.s. I'm sending back the signed divorce papers and all of the letters you've sent me during this hard time. I'll gladly keep all the rest, but I don't think I can even stand the sight of these letters because I'll know that they were the end of something that should've been more. Please don't send me another letter. Let's just leave it at this.

I bundled them up with twine after reading them again. They had served their purpose. I texted a picture of them to Jax and asked if he wanted to read them with me.

"Never thought I'd say this and mean it, but yeah. I do actually."

"Let me know when you're ready."

"Can I come pick you up this evening? We can go back to the lake. That feels like a sacred place for us. Our hallowed ground so to speak."

"Let me know what time and I'll be ready."

CHAPTER THIRTEEN
EMBERS OF HEALING
AGE 23

Marley:

He came to pick me up around 7 that evening. We grabbed some dinner and drove back to the lake, the silence in the car carrying all the weight of the sorrow we were about to let go of. When we got out of the car, Jackson set up a chair for me and went to find some fallen branches to start a fire - the one thing I had requested. His pace, harried and just hair away from frantic. His face, stoic and serious, but he took great care in getting the fire up and rolling. The heat of the blaze felt warm on the side of my body that was closest to it. The other side still felt the crisp air of that late spring evening. The juxtaposition felt poetic given what we were about to do.

Once he was sure that the fire was underway, he

pulled a chair up beside me and plopped down in it, his face already painted with the universal expression of loss. I reached out for his hand and gazed at the flickering light reflecting off his smooth brown skin. The bonfire crackled and popped, its dancing flames mirrored the turbulent emotions within our hearts. The leaves applauded our courageous act as the wind rustled them up. The water lapping up against the shoreline seemingly shushed to soothe our grief. Life had dealt us a cruel hand, but fate had placed us in a prime position to heal.

Jax:
The pain I had tried to bury deep within my soul was demanding to be acknowledged, to be grieved, and I was finally ready to face it with Marley. I had gone to therapy individually, but I felt like we never got to grieve together. This was our chance. As the sun began its descent, casting a fiery haze across the horizon, Marley gently squeezed my hand, offering me silent reassurance. It was exactly the touch of unwavering support and a commitment to share my pain and carry it alongside her own that I didn't even know I needed.

"When I read these letters, it feels like yesterday, Jackson." I could see the pain in her eyes as she gazed at my face. Those eyes that usually melted me to my core, had finally evoked a different emotion from me. "It's still there, hanging out with me. I feel like I've carried the weight of our loss all these years, but seeing the tears in your eyes, I know you carried it with you too. Each in our own way, but this is the first time we don't have to face it alone anymore."

The tears rolled from my eyes with a ferociousness I'd never experienced before. "I'm so sorry I wasn't there to help you through it, Marley. I should've left training. I should've come to see you. To be with you. To sit with you. To cry with you."

"It's okay, Jackson."

"It's not. I stayed in training so I could get a good job and take care of you. Take care of us. I was doing it for us, but I didn't realize that what I was working towards would be nonexistent if I couldn't be present in the moment. Everything was for our future, but I missed the moments that mattered, especially the moment you needed me most. I think about it every day, Marley."

Her words tinged with sorrow and tenderness, matched the softness of the evening breeze. "Jackson, you were grieving too. I didn't understand it at the time, but after reading these letters again I see it now."

"Marley, I've carried his memory within me every single day. I've tried to heal by myself but our grief, our love, they're meant to be shared."

She stood up and welcomed me into the warmth of her arms. The air was alive with the scent of the crackling wood and the promise of catharsis. In her hands she held the letters we had written to each other during that window of dreams deferred and grief untamed.

"I'm right here, Ring Bearer. I'm right here." I buried my head into her shoulder and sobbed. I had mostly held in my grief for more than 2000 days. That's 2000 days of anger, frustration, sorrow, guilt, despair. I crumpled into her arms. "You're so strong, Jax," she whispered into my ear. I felt the exact opposite of that in the moment. "It's one of the reasons I've loved you all this time. It's okay for a strong man to need a spotter. It's also okay for a strong man to set the weight down. If you don't, your muscles will get worn out. Let me know which one you need right now."

I could barely get the words out, "I just need this. I just need you, Marley."

She nodded. "Are you sure you're ready to read these?" Marley asked, tapping my back with the envelopes.

"Yes. I'm ready." I told her, easing out of her embrace.

With a trembling hand I took the stack of letters from Marley and sifted through them, handing those addressed to me back to her, and keeping those with my handwriting on them. We read them aloud in sequence. Each letter got progressively more difficult to read as time wore on. By the time we reached the end, I was out of tears. I mistakenly thought I had cried them all out. Marley walked closer to the fire looking deeply at the address on the front of the first envelope. With one deep breath in, she faced the pain head-on and placed the letter into the fire.

I watched as the flames hungrily devoured the paper, then followed suit, tears flowing as freely as when we read the letters we had written again. The expressions of love and loss all transformed into ashes. We alternated between the release of our letters. As the flames consumed our words, a sense of long overdue relief washed over me. For each letter dropped into the flames, a 10 pound burden was lifted from my shoulders and the weight of my grief became much more manageable and less binding. Marley leaned into me with the last letter, her head resting against my shoulder the way she so often did. The last letter in her hand was unopened and she handed it to me, asking me to read it aloud.

Dear Ring Bearer,

I know you asked me not to write you anymore, but you're the one person I want to talk to most in this moment, and the one person I can't. I don't know if you'll ever receive this because I'm not supposed to send it, but I need to get these feelings out.

Earlier this year I got engaged to my best friend and the person I adored most in this world. It was THE happiest moment in my life so far. We knew we wanted to be together but I moved away to college and he got accepted into a competitive cybersecurity program which meant his training would take him off grid for 6 months. We didn't have any plans to get married or start a family right away so it was okay. All of that was planned for years down the road when I was closer to graduation. I knew how strong our love was and I never questioned whether or not marriage was the right decision once we found out that God had other plans for us. It was a simple ceremony that felt so much like us - no frills, no fuss - just love. I didn't know His plans would involve so much joy and despair.

We were going to have a baby. I called them Junior. But Junior's spirit was too pure for this world and their mission I think, was to help us - to help me remember that we all have a purpose here.

My world has turned upside down and I need you to know, Ring Bearer, that your steady love throughout the years is helping to make things less topsy turvy. Not many things make much sense anymore. After we lost Junior, it all came undone. Our marriage fell apart. I lost my best friend. I even lost myself for a moment. Sometimes though, things require an unraveling to become stronger. I think, I hope this is one of those times.

I know that this love isn't really gone. Somewhere nestled deep within my heart I know that we'll find our way back to each other. We'll have a moment to grieve together and we'll begin to rebuild our lives. I love him dearly and I hope he knows that my decision to end things was only made so we didn't tear each other down or destroy each other in our grief. We can't miss what's never gone. No matter how long it takes, I'm willing to wait for him. He has my heart forever. We'll be back before too long.

I will always love you, Ring Bearer. Jax. Jackson. Groom. If you get a chance to read this it means that time has gifted us another chance to heal together and I'm forever grateful for it - and for you.

Love and cherish you always,
Mar

p.s. Please don't burn this one.

I folded the letter up and stuffed it into my pocket. The fire cast a warm comforting glow on her hopeful face. There was so much left unsaid that lingered in the cool night air. I don't know that I'd ever wept so much in my life. I finally whispered a question into the ether, my voice still caught in my throat.

"Can I kiss you, Mar?" Our eyes were locked. Our hearts were loaded. And my love, after gently caressing my face, she pulled me closer and kissed me like tomorrow may never come. It breathed life back into my body. "Always my girl, Marley."

"Always, Jax?"

"Since we were 8 years old - the moment I first laid eyes on you."

"How did you know?"

"I think it was your light."

"I love you so much, Jackson. Thank you for today."

Marley:

As the stars made their appearance that night, the two of us continued to nestle with each other near the bonfire, basking in the tender embrace of that evening. The flames danced on, whispering secrets of healing and hope as our hearts began to mend together, one ember at a time.

That lake had witnessed the spark of our love, the depths of our grief, and also our resilience and strength. What once was, had turned to ashes, and slowly but surely from the ashes, together we had embraced the promise of a future where love and hope would take root again.

CHAPTER FOURTEEN
LOVE UNLEASHED
AGE 23

Jax:

That night at the lake was healing in ways I didn't even know I needed to be healed. I had been frustrated with my Godmother for putting me back in the same space as the woman who broke my heart. I had been angsty. I wasn't sure how to funnel all of those feelings that came rushing back. But that night at the lake...the tears, that kiss. That kiss. That. Kiss.

I always knew she was the one, but the way she cared for my heart when it was clear that hers was still being pieced back together too - that lit a fire under me. I didn't think things could go back to where they were, but I was sure that the future held something much stronger because of that kiss. I wanted to take things slowly this time. We had eternity in my mind so there wasn't really a need to rush into marriage again. Plus, there was a new wrinkle that I needed to share with Marley.

Marley:

He moved at the pace of a turtle. I didn't understand it. Time and some very persistent people in our lives had put us back in touch after 5 years of silence. Five years. I was so eager to be in his presence again. I was eager to be his girl again. I was eager to spend every day with him. But he took 5 days to call me after the lake. I didn't want to push him away but I didn't want to fall into another 5 year lapse either. I was sure about him and I needed reassurance that he was sure about me. Well, I wanted reassurance, I guess I didn't really need it.

Either way I was direct with him as he took me to a rooftop park, hidden away in plain sight in downtown Kansas City. We sat on a bench underneath a small shade tree looking out at the tops of the buildings in the city. My mind awash with anxiety. My body full of nervous energy. Jackson had made and packed lunch for us. I twirled my fork in the cold spaghetti salad over and over, rolling the black olives around on the paper plate, trying to choose my words and timing very carefully.

"Jackson..." I quietly started

"Is the food okay, Mar?" he asked with slight concern in his voice as he stared at the obstacle course of noodles I had created on my plate.

I twirled some onto my fork and took a bite. "It's delicious, Jax."

He nodded then studied my face. "You okay, Marley?"

"I'm just...I want you to know..." I hesitated twice, trying to get the words to come out just right.

"Just let it out, you can fix it if you don't say what you really mean. What do you want me to know?"

I mustered up as much determination as I could and tried again, "Jackson, I love you more than words can express, and this still feels right to me - we still feel right to me. Sometimes it feels like we have our own language and understanding." I heaved out all the air in my lungs then took a long cleansing inhale and told him what I wanted to know. "I've been wondering where WE stand in your mind."

Jackson softly held my hands and gazed into my eyes. His so soft. So sincere. His words, powerful and few. "Marley, we're still married in my heart. You remember the last letter I wrote to you? I meant that. We're not legally married anymore, but it never stopped the love."

I nodded, hearing the words he was speaking but one question still lingered in my heart. "What happened between the bonfire and when you reached out to me again?"

"I was overthinking everything," he paused, his head in his hands, looking like he was trying to find the right words. Before he spoke again, he sat upright, turning his body to face me, his eyes so sincere, "I want the next time we get married to be the last time we get married, Marley. I rushed everything when we were younger. I was so excited to get married to you and start a family with you that I let the illusion overshadow reality. I don't want the illusion anymore because I know after these last few days that the reality is far better. But I do want to take it slowly. We already have forever, Marley. We're just building a stronger foundation for this house."

I knew exactly what he meant and my heart was

reassured. I snuggled up into his arms, my mind and body now at ease, and took a quick nap. We could build a house anywhere with a strong foundation, but Jax was my home.

That nap was short-lived. I awoke to the feeling of a cold, wet nose, rubbing up against my hand. I instinctively knew it wasn't Jackson, which caused even more of a startle. It had to be a dog. I was still terrified of them. I opened my eyes, recoiled my hand and immediately yelped, which startled Jackson awake. It also startled the dog, who looked at me with confused eyes like it was just trying to say hello.

"Whoa there, little one," Jackson said as he called for the dog to come closer to him and immediately looked around for someone with a broken leash. He checked for a chip or any type of id, but didn't seem to find anything. "How you doing, Marley?" he asked softly.

I exhaled slowly through pursed lips and nodded slowly in his direction.

"You're okay. Just be. Juuust be."

I nodded and worked on my breath, remembering the look in the eyes of the dog. I lowered my eyes back in the direction of the dog that had settled in with Jax. The wagging tail and tongue wags let me know it was excitedly soaking up his snuggles and petting. It gradually turned its head in my direction, catching my eye, and slowly with a bowed head walked over to me, as if to see if I was okay. I guess that was something to be expected the way I had just yelped.

It rested its head on my lap and whimpered. Jackson reached over and rubbed behind the pooch's ear while softly checking on me. "He seems to like you, Marley. How do you feel about him? Are you ready to go or do you want to sit here with him for a while?"

I exhaled, surprised at the answer that came out of my mouth. "I'm doing okay. I think I want to sit here for a while, Jackson." An energized smile spread across his face. He looked equally proud of me and also eager for the moment we were sharing together.

"Do you want to pet him?" He asked, stretching out his hand for mine. I nodded and Jackson lowered our hands softly onto the dog's head. "Feel how soft his fur is?" I was amazed at how quickly I was adapting. After being chased home by a doberman everyday after school in 4th grade, I didn't think I'd ever want to be around dogs again. They all scared me - yet there I was, with Jax, working through the mental barriers I had created for myself. "You're doing so good, Mar," he spoke ever so calmly. He took out his phone and took a picture of me gazing down at the dog that looked so lovingly up in my direction.

"What do I do, Jackson?" I asked him.

He voice held a bit of angst, "Are you ready to go, Marley?"

"No, I wanna keep him." My words even shocked me. I looked up at Jax, awaiting his answer but the words just hung out in the back of his mouth which had fallen open wide enough for flies to invite themselves inside.

"This dog?" he asked with shock.

I nodded. The fear I had held onto so tightly transformed, my heart beginning to swell with affection for the 4 legged pooch who still rested his precious little face on my lap.

"Jackson?"

He was stunned into near silence. "You're incredible. You know that?" He said as he leaned in and kissed the crown of my head. "Maybe we should see if he belongs to someone first."

He stood to his feet and my buddy lifted his head from

my lap, suddenly looking in Jax's direction. Jax, snapped a finger and my buddy stood to his feet beside the man that I loved so deeply and could suddenly see in an all new light.

"Marley..." Jackson's words lingered into the cool night air.

"Yes, Jackson?" I asked while still looking lovingly at my buddy, the dog that had just mysteriously found his way to me.

"I gotta be honest. I know this dog's owner."

"Huh?"

He stooped down in front of the dog and asked it to go grab its leash. The dog took off, running to the other side of the park and came back holding a leash in its mouth.

"That was pretty incredible."

"So, this is Buddy. He's my dog. I'm not sure how he got off of his leash though. He was supposed to be with a dog walker, but I don't see them anywhere around here."

It was my turn to be stunned. This curly-maned pooch that I loved almost instantaneously belonged to my ex-husband. Now there's a shocker.

"You got a dog, Jackson? You always wanted one!"

"I did. But I wasn't gonna get one if it made you uncomfortable." He lowered his eyes to my buddy - his Buddy, before continuing, "Then we didn't make it and I needed something to funnel my love towards. Enter Buddy and all his lovable goofiness. He played a pretty big role in helping me heal."

I was amazed.

"I knew when we cursed each other out on the phone that I needed some deep healing. You didn't deserve any of that and I didn't have a place for my love to go anymore. My therapist recommended a dog. I was just out on my way to work one day and there he was, lost and looking abandoned by the side of the road. I promised myself if he was still there on my lunch break that I'd get him and go see if someone had lost him. When he was still there, I went to the closest animal shelter and they couldn't find a chip or any record of him, so he became My Buddy."

I stared in awe at his transformation. Now recognizing it was because of the unconditional love that they were able to share with each other that likely helped Jackson open up more to me. I loved Buddy even more.

"Also, I'm sorry he startled you awake, and that you were introduced to him this way. I wasn't expecting him to be out here and I definitely didn't know he would take to you so quickly," he finished as he secured the leash around his collar.

I leaned down to pet Buddy as I encouraged Jackson back into a standing position. "Can I walk him home?"

"I love you so much, Marley."

"Soooo, is that a yes then?"

He kissed my head and nodded, handing me the leash. I didn't know where I was leading him, but Buddy walked faithfully between the two of us as Jackson led us to the elevator and down to apartment 909.

He unlocked the door and let Buddy zoom inside. While Buddy was busy inspecting the apartment, Jackson took a moment to ask me a question. "I don't want to seem too forward or eager. You're more than welcome to come inside now, or I can take you home and we can plan another time for you to come hang out inside. Which would you prefer, Sweetheart?"

I opened the door and peeked inside, looking for Buddy, who quickly zoomed back to the front door like he was waiting to show me something. "May I?" I asked, Jackson.

He motioned like he was welcoming me inside.

I stepped through the door and Buddy wriggled onto my legs as I walked towards the couch in the living room.

"I'll grab you some water, Marley."

"Thank you, Jackson. Can we watch the live action version of Lady and the Tramp again?"

He chuckled, "Whatever you'd like ma'am."

"I didn't really get to watch that the last time since the kids were so busy falling asleep and whatnot."

He paused on his way to the kitchen and made an about face. "You remember that?"

"I hold that memory close to my heart, Jax. That's the moment my heart really opened up."

An uncontrollable grin spread across his face. "Let me go grab that water."

We watched the movie all snuggled up with each other in the same way that we had 7 years before. This time, instead of one of his god siblings laying on me, it was Buddy - who also fell asleep on my lap.

In that moment I was grateful for patience, and openness, and honesty, and I was surprisingly grateful for the dog who felt like he was there to remind us both of the importance of unconditional love and second chances. It seemed nonsensical to say it out loud, but I felt the presence of the child we lost there within Buddy. And in that moment I felt reassured that all would be okay including our future, which I knew deep within we were laying a foundation for. That foundation was filled with the promise of a love that would be stronger and more resilient than ever before.

Jax:

Sitting with Marley on that old wooden bench in the

park, I was nervous. I was excited. I was still in love with her. It had been a rollercoaster since we reconnected after our divorce, annulment, whatever you want to call it, and at 23, we were rediscovering what we had lost.

The conversation we just had lingered in the air, and I could see the vulnerability in Marley's eyes as she asked me why I was taking my time to get back into a relationship. The truth was I didn't have any doubts. Our love was strong, I just didn't want to rush into it like I had the first time through. Being with her felt so right and I didn't want to let fear hold me back.

She nodded understandingly and I couldn't help but feel a spark of hope.

As the evening turned into a tranquil dusk, the warm breeze wrapped around us like a blanket. Our conversation had been heavy and our emotions had been running full cylinder. Both had taken their toll on us and we ended up dozing off on the bench. I felt so content, so at home with Marley's head resting gently on my shoulder.

In the midst of our peaceful nap, the serenity of the park was shattered by the sudden appearance of an unexpected guest. Marley's yelp jolted me awake. I looked in her direction to see if she was okay. The fear was evident in her eyes as she felt a dog's nose on her hand. I quickly tried to reassure her that everything was okay, but her fear of dogs was deeply rooted.

"Just be," I said, trying to soothe her anxiety. "Juuuuust be."

I knew for certain that the Bernedoodle which had startled her awake was a friendly one even though Marley didn't know that. I called him over to me to give her some space, then checked in to see what she wanted to do next, all the while searching for the person who was supposed to be watching my dog. I hadn't meant for them to meet like that. I wanted to ease her into an introduction to this goofy guy, not throw her into the deep end and ask her to swim without any lessons or heads up.

But, we were already in the moment, so I had to think quickly. I invited Marley to pet him and we approached it slowly. To my surprise, she allowed me to take her hand and guide her through the process. My dog responded warmly. I couldn't help but admire Marley's bravery in facing her fear head on - literally.

When she told me she wanted to keep him I froze. I thought this might've been a deal breaker and there she was asking me what to do because she could feel the love that Buddy gives so freely to my friends and family. Once I had eased out of my state of shock, I fessed up to owning the dog that she had been calling by name without realizing it. I told her about how we met; how he saved me and loved me into a better version of myself. Then Marley just stared at me. It felt like I waited an eternity to see her again, then she was back in my life and pushing through her deepest fears to love on this dog, my dog. She asked to walk him home and I handed her the leash I had sent Buddy to retrieve.

I thought I already loved her deeply, but watching her walk him with so much joy awakened another part of me that I thought I had turned off when our family fell to pieces. I didn't want her to feel obligated to come into my apartment when we arrived, but I hoped that she wanted to. I still wanted to move slowly, but this new version of me had so much love to share and I wanted to be around her.

We watched "Lady and the Tramp," that night, per her request. It brought back memories of that night we watched my godsibs. We'd come so far since then. But this time when I asked if I could kiss her, she welcomed it. My body responded like I was still 16, but I reminded myself to slow down. I could feel deep down in my bones that this love was forever. I wanted to cherish each day instead of rushing to get to some finish line, like marriage or kids, or whatever came with it.

As we hung out on the couch, Marley nestled under my arm and Buddy sleeping on her lap, I began to wonder if this was what a second chance at love was all about. That night I felt so grateful for the way things had fallen into place.

As the days turned into weeks and the weeks into months, Marley and I found ourselves growing ever comfortable in each other's presence. We began to share responsibility for Buddy. When I had to travel for work, she would come stay at my place and take care of him until I returned. That shared nurturing only deepened our connection.

I remembered a conversation I'd had with her Dad, back before I graduated from high school and had asked for his blessing to marry his daughter. He asked if I was ready to commit to only one person for the rest of my life and I told him that I had already only committed to one person for my life. He told me to, "Ask her when you feel it in your heart, when you love her as she is, when you know for certain that you can add light to the world together."

After 9 months of dating slowly, I felt it. I loved her all day long, but most of all in the evening time when she was just about out of energy for the day. There was a softness about her that was more present than when she woke up to start the day or even when she was snuggling in next to me. In her soft hour, she was the most honest and blunt, she let her hair down and her master's degree candidate nature went out the window. In her soft hour, we'd collaborate on things to make each other better and big ideas that would create endless ripples of impact around us. I knew in my gut when I was going to propose again, it was going to be during that hour. All that remained was for me to pick the right day.

CHAPTER FIFTEEN
LOVE'S BEST FRIEND
AGE 24

Marley:

Remember when I told you that the totality of our relationship hinges on one very simplistic fact? The energy you put into the atmosphere always finds its way back to you. I was patient and kind when it came to Jackson and our second chance at love. Our world wasn't always easy going, but the bumps we faced together were definitely easier because he was also patient and kind when it came to me - to us.

Jackson had been a constant in my life since I was 7 years old. He'll tell you since we were 8, but he just doesn't understand how pivotal his peace dove was in my recovery from brain surgery. Maybe he thinks I'm just exaggerating, but I literally read it everyday. His words poured into me everyday. They nursed my mind, my heart, and my emotions while the medical staff tended to my body. I have loved this man and his pure heart since what felt like the beginning of time.

I gazed at him as we sat on the couch that night and marveled at how far we'd come. I found myself surveying random odd parts, his calves, his fingernails, his elbows. I was taking in all the details until my eyes found their way up to his. He was already in the process of returning my loving stare by the time my eyes arrived at their final destination. I loved looking into his eyes. It helped me to have a better sense of what he was feeling internally and sometimes, when I was exhausted by the day - his eyes transported me to another world. When I looked into them that night, there was a level of contentment that hadn't been present before.

Don't get me wrong, I'd seen contentment in his eyes before, but this look felt like an understanding that this is what the future would hold - quiet nights that followed on the heels of days where we were co-existing in the same space, working together towards a big audacious goal, and sometimes just snuggling on the couch with his dog. I don't remember saying anything, just nodding in agreeance with the deep contentment and appreciation for where we were in life.

A wave of comfort rolled over me. I closed my eyes to stretch my body and let out a lingering yawn. Jackson's face lit up as he watched me contort until I was totally relaxed.

He snapped his finger and called Buddy over to the couch where the two of us were seated side by side. Buddy placed his face on the couch between us and Jackson rubbed the top of his head and gave him a command.

"Do me a favor, Buddy."

Buddy raised upright as tall as he could manage while still on all fours. There was something dangling from his collar.

"Jackson, what's that on his collar?" I asked as he reached down and unhooked it. Jackson, in his crew length socks, gym shorts and a t shirt, got off the couch and crouched down on one knee in front of me, Buddy still beside him. He handed me the box but held onto my hands while he spoke.

"Marley, the last time I got down on one knee in front of you it was to ask you to marry me. I didn't know it at the time, but in spite of the lessons I'd received from my godfather, I had no idea how to be a good husband to you. I thought I knew everything there was to know. Life quickly taught me that I only know a fraction of a fraction of half a percent of all the knowledge that exists in this universe, including how to be a good life partner - but I'm open to learn.

I have loved you for two thirds of my life and spending the last year of it with you has been far better than anything I imagined for our first marriage. I'm so grateful that you're here and I love the life we're building together - Buddy included." He reached down to pet his pooch who was staring up at me as if he were also asking for my hand in marriage. Jackson continued, "This guy helped me heal from heartbreak. He helped you heal a deep fear. He also helped us learn what it means to function as a family and I owe him greatly for bringing us closer than ever.

Marley, you are a fighter. Remember you are strong even when you don't feel like it. I also hope you know that you can be soft and lay your burdens down with me. You've shown me what it means to love and be loved. You've brought so much happiness and contentment into my life and I can't imagine a future without you in it. Would you be willing to give our marriage another shot? Can we get married again?"

I had rivers of tears flowing down my cheeks by the time he finished. My hair was up in a messy bun and I had my glasses on. I thought I was about to tell him goodnight and go lay down in his bed. Instead I found myself staring through blurred vision at the man who had just bared his soul and asked me to marry him again.

I was thinking about his first proposal, and the beautiful ceremony we had for our quickie wedding, and the loss that ruptured our bond. I wondered about the future and what our family would look like aside from the three of us, and what would happen if we were to find ourselves in a similar situation again. I was lost in the past and trying to sort out the future before it happened.

Jackson reached out and softly held my cheek in his hand, his thumb tracing the tracks of my tears, "Marley, breathe with me Sweetheart."

I nodded and held onto the hand that was comforting me. The box, still closed, was in my other hand. One slow inhale brought me back to the present moment. "I can't imagine a life without you in it either."

"Can we try again?" he asked once more.

I leaned in and excitedly kissed him. "Yes, Jackson!! Of course we can!"

He opened the box and presented me with a new ring - one that was custom made for me. It was gorgeous. He slipped it on my finger and kissed me with depth and passion that flipped my world upside down. It had been one of the most ordinary evenings turned extraordinary with Jax's surprise proposal, and I soon learned that he was just getting started.

"I have something else to show you, Mar," he eagerly said while signaling to Buddy who went into his kennel and returned holding in his mouth a ribbon attached to a small box. Within the box were cocktail napkins from an airplane. All held wishes for the future Jax and I had tried to build the first go round.

"These messages," he explained, "were written when we were young. I was going to give you one each week when we finally got to live in the same space together. The timing now feels more poetic given all that we've experienced together."

We read them all slowly, one at a time, until we'd completed nearly 100 letters. About the same amount remained unread, but Jax sent Buddy into the bedroom for one more thing. He returned with an envelope - with my name on it.

I thanked Buddy, who smiled at me, appreciative of the snuggles he had just received. I ran my finger underneath the seal, opening the envelope to find a card with a handwritten message - not in Jackson's handwriting, and one single rose petal with the letter M on it, in my handwriting. It was the rose petal I had returned to Jax all those years ago. He did say he'd keep it forever.

I smiled at the rose petal and pulled the card closer to read it.

> Dear Marley,
>
> You've been the best mom to me and I
> love you more than Jackson does. I cry
> when you're not here and my wags grow
> in happiness when you're with us. Will you
> marry me too so our family is complete?
>
> Buddy

I didn't know a proposal from a dog would make me cry the way it did. Something about being called his mom triggered the return of the sense that this dog had the same energy as the child I once carried.

The totality of our relationship hinges on one very simplistic fact. The energy you put into the atmosphere always finds its way back to you. I loved Jax and Buddy with my whole heart, and all the energy of love and gratitude that I put out into the world got returned to me ten-fold.

Our love was boundless as was the promise of all that could be. My childhood sweetheart was the forever love I had envisioned and Buddy our supernatural guardian. Time had only deepened our love and I was grateful for the steadfast energy Jackson used to water our relationship. I could hardly wait to see what we would harvest.

AUTHOR'S NOTES & ACKNOWLEDGEMENTS

Author's Notes

From the last Author's Notes:

"Only time will tell whether or not I continue to write romance novels. But, the stories within the Sugarplum series have had a profound and indelible impact on my life. They've taught me more about myself, about life, and about love. So I guess I did write the story that I needed afterall. For that I am exceedingly grateful."

Well, I'm still writing romance novels. I thought, no - maybe I hoped that the first three in the series were going to be the only ones, but I think deep down I knew that there were more. Significantly more. The truth, the whole truth, and nothing but the truth is there are far more stories bubbling. This is the first in the story of Marley & Jax. The other characters also have stories to tell as well. We know a little bit about Sabrina and Steve (Jax's parents) but their story - specifically the mystery behind their absense during Jax's high school years is a doozy. There was a teaser of another love story in this one that I'm hoping you caught. And don't think we're leaving out Oakley...she may need her own separate series.

This story, like most of the stories in the Sugarplum Universe is all about trusting what you feel and being willing to pour love in the world in spite of hurt, disappointment, and potential fear. The desire to fold and crumple or disappear may be present, but so much joy is around us if we're willing to look for it, if we're willing to create it, if we're willing to live within a space where multiple things can be true at once.

Loss is a heavy, painful thing to navigate and it's so hard to write about. But the undoing created by loss, leaves us with an opportunity to reconnect with what's truly important to us.

This series was an unexpected detour from my path as a children's book author, and one I have learned to embrace over time. They say authors write the stories that they need, yet I doubted that I needed a romance novel in my life. I was wrong.

These books were about so much more than Marley, Jax, Dr. Chris, Charlie, Marlo, Steve, Sabrina, and any of the other characters who are included. They're far bigger than romance. They're about the sweet fruit that comes from nurturing healthy relationships; romantic, friendly, familial, collegial, whatever form.

Even when we think we have the answer, we only really possess a tiny fraction of knowledge compared to all the information there is to obtain. Through these books I've had the chance to connect more interpersonally with readers and friends, and while none of it was something I predicted for my life, I am grateful for every ounce of it.

Acknowledgements

To the Beta Readers, your patience, quick follow through and time is truly invaluable. I appreciate your willingness to ensure that this next book in the Sugarplum Universe lives up to the expectations left by the first three books in the series. I appreciate you more than you know.

To the friends and family who encouraged me to listen and share, I appreciate you and am tremendously grateful for your support. My most sincere thanks to the crew (you know who you are). I appreciate your time, your honest critiques, and the humor you leant to my writing process. Thanks for ensuring I remained human throughout the writing of this story.

To Kelly & T, who are unknowingly - unless they read this - two of the greatest examples of how to navigate through some of the most difficult situations while still showing up for others and not losing themselves in the process, Thank You, thank you, thank you, a million times over for holding space for me when I needed it most. Know that your friendship is one in a million and the same is always here for you, regardless of the circumstances.

To Coach, thanks for the inspiration to finish this story. I came to you for help pushing through my own fear of dogs and you asked me to add two to this story. I only added one because I'm obstinate...kidding - kind of. It felt more poignant to this story to just have one and it helped me further reframe how I see dogs. Always grateful for your extra push and your light.

To The Elmores, thank you for the detour around the Baltimore Harbour on my way to the airport, and for every other way you've poured into my life. They say friends are the family we choose - I agree 100%.

To my parents, siblings, and relatives, thank you for showing me what family can mean, in all its varied examples. It is because of how you love each other and others that I can write a story that displays grace and grit, and how to build long lasting relationships. I love you to the moon and back!

Finally, to the enthusiatic readers of the Sugarplum series, thank you for sharing your love of Dr. Chris and Charlie. I hope this next iteration lives up to the hype. If this is your first foray into the Sugarplum Series, welcome. Now that you've finished this book, you might give A Spoonful of Sugarplums a chance. It will help to fill in some of the details for you.

Remember always, there is at least one thing exists without beginning or end. Love is eternal.

ABOUT THE AUTHOR

C. L. Fails is an author, story shepherd, joy sherpa, and an accidental educator; having served pre-school through college students in her hometown of Kansas City. An agent for equity, she has dedicated her career to helping others learn to follow their internal compass, and thrive despite challenge. She is currently Founder & CEO of LaunchCrate Publishing - a company created to help writers launch their work into the world while retaining the portion of profit they deserve. Outside of LaunchCrate she is an active advocate for education, serving as a former Girls on the Run Coach, on the Board of Directors for several nonprofits and is highly involved with several equity initiatives through her collegiate alma mater.

She is author of several books that inspire us to be bold, take risks, and learn from our mistakes. When she's not helping clients, hosting a podcast, speaking with audiences or working on her latest work in progress about building community, you can find her doodling on whatever object may be nearby.

Her favorite work is documenting personal narratives through the Modern Memoir service, and serving as a Story Shepherd to writers, working to launch their work into the world through Idea to Editor. Both services are offered by LaunchCrate Publishing. Check out launchcrate.com for more detailed information.

9 781947 506367